Karin,
Welcome to
Freedom Valle!

D1489669

All Inn Thyme

ERIN BRANSCOM

I hope you
love Mellie's Tey
as much as I do!

Erin

Mom and Dad,
Thanks for being our shelter from our storm. The memories
the boys and I made with you will always be treasured.
You reminded us we are special, safe, and loved.

This book contains heavy-hearted content pertaining to domestic violence. As an author, I think pieces of us are sprinkled into every story that we write. We write what we know and we write to heal. This book is dedicated to anyone who has struggled or knows someone who has struggled with domestic violence. I hope this book finds anyone who needs it. You deserve to be safe and loved. You're not alone. We're in this world together.

Love, Erin

And for all the "Bradley's" out there...
I hope you step on a Lego.

All Inn Thyme

CHAPTER 1

~

Mellie

I had no idea what he was fixing,
but mine was broken.

When I got married five years ago, I pictured a dream life
with a beautiful cozy home, a family sharing loud dinners,
belly laughs during game nights, and fun vacations to the
beach or the mountains.

That's not even close to the hell that I got.

Now, my son and I are truly *living* in a cozy loft above a
garden shed behind a family-owned inn in New Hampshire.
Our entire living space could probably fit into the kitchen of
our old home, but at least we're safe now. My son and I have

been through so much, but we've made it out.

Deep breaths. Deep breaths.

We're safe in Freedom Valley. We're not in Mississippi anymore.

Breathe, Mellie. Breathe. In and out.

I turn to scan my garden as I focus on my breaths. I clench my fist and run my knuckles over my chest, trying to ease the tightness.

A sense of warmth comes over me like a wave as I take in the rows of dirt, seeds planted under the dark soil by my very own hands, and growth beginning to sprout. The sun heats my back as I take in the colors—pops of dark and light greens and brown dirt, wet from the rain. The rich garden aroma brings me back to where I truly am, and not what makes me anxious. This is my safe space. The place where I can think and finally dream again.

I make my way back to the inn and look down at my clothes streaked in dirt. I need to shower before dinner, and I still have some laundry to catch up on. I need to get my linen carts stocked for tomorrow so I can hit the ground running and free up more time to garden.

I step into the shed and find Beth, who's become one of my best friends this past year. She's been through her own hell, and she knows some of my story, but not a lot. When her fiancé Evan, the owner of the inn, brought my son and me here to the Golden Gable, he agreed to keep my past a secret, and so far, we've done that. Beth helps out wherever needed, and to my confusion, she actually likes doing the laundry, so that works out for both of us.

"We're almost ready to eat. Sasha's made an Italian-themed feast for dinner: stuffed shells, homemade garlic bread from Allie, a huge garden salad, and tiramisu for dessert." She rubs her small baby belly bump with one hand and continues to fold towels with the other. "It smells so amazing in that kitchen. I can't get enough garlic with this pregnancy."

My stomach growls as if in agreement. "I'm starved. I haven't eaten since breakfast."

Beth's face scrunches up in worry. "You need to make sure you're taking care of yourself. You're working too hard."

I know she's right, but the garden isn't work to me, it's my therapy. "How have you been feeling?" I ask, changing the subject.

"I'm finally past all the morning sickness and now I just feel tired sometimes, but I'm mostly doing great. I can't believe we're really having a baby. Evan is over the moon. He barely lets me lift a finger."

I chuckle at Evan's overprotectiveness. "I bet. He's so good with Kase, I know he's going to be such a good dad."

Beth looks around. "Speaking of, where's Kase?"

"He just left with Logan and Allie to play with Caleb."

"Why don't you go take a quick shower and I'll finish up."

She looks around, her face taking on a look of dismay.

"What?" I laugh as she scans the chaos of the space.

"I wasn't going to say anything, but honestly, the garden shed is feeling more like an actual garden shed these days." She laughs as she stacks a neat pile of towels onto the cart.

She's not wrong. Every surface available is covered in starter plants under grow lights as I get ready for our spring planting. I have papers taped to the walls with colorful hand-drawn diagrams of where everything will be planted in the new gardens I already set up at the back of the property. Over the past year, I have been able to explore my passion for gardening, and I feel like I've finally found my purpose. When I'm not cleaning rooms at the inn or taking care of Kase, I'm reading gardening books, watching plant videos on YouTube, or researching new things to grow. It's become a big part of my healing. When I'm with the plants, I have peace.

The garden shed, as everyone calls it, is actually a cool "barndominium"—a small barn with two levels. The stairs on the side lead to a small studio apartment I've made cozy with thrifted finds, DIY crafts, and a revolving selection of books I check out from the library—plus more plants. All things that make me feel cozy and happy.

I do feel a bit guilty, though, for taking over the laundry space with my plants, and I tell Beth, "I know. I'm sorry. As soon as I can get my greenhouse together, all of this will go out there."

"Oh, I don't mind it. It's kind of cool, Mellie. I love seeing you so happy with all your plants. You've really, um, blossomed." She says the last part with an exaggerated wink.

"You and your dad jokes." I laugh, shaking my head.

"Yeah, and you love me." She pulls me into a side hug.

"That I do," I say as I hug her back.

"Okay, don't make me get all sappy. Go take your shower. These hormones are all over the place and I cry at everything these days."

"Thank you," I call as I quickly jog up the stairs.

We had a lot of guest turnover today and I worked hard to get all the rooms fresh and ready before putting in a good hour outside. I'm exhausted and sweaty, so much so that I think I can smell myself at this point. I wish I could crawl under the covers and go straight to bed, but that's not a possibility.

Beth doesn't know that every single surface up here is covered in plants, as well. I quickly move the ones from my shower, perched on the overhead window, basking in natural light.

Once I'm showered and clean, I grab a t-shirt and my better pair of jeans from a basket on the floor. I don't even own enough clothes to put away. I wash and re-wear everything practically daily, and mostly I wear older clothes to clean and garden in. Who cares about clothes when you can buy more seeds and plants?

I gave up on caring how I look a while ago. I just want to be comfortable and have my hands in the dirt. My eyes roam over my plants as I quickly dry my hair and pull it back. I can't wait to see them thriving outside as they grow into fresh veggies for us to eat.

Spring is here and it feels so good outside as I head over to the main house, thankful for some good food and family time. No, I'm not related to these people, but they have all gone out of their way to make me and Kase feel like we're part of their family, blood or not. I ease in the back door, looking around. The sounds of chatter and the smells of garlic and Italian food greet me, my mouth instantly watering.

"There you are," Margie says in a motherly tone. Evan and Allie's mom beams as she comes over and pulls me close. "We waited for you," she says as she guides me into the kitchen and hands me a glass of wine.

Warmth spreads through my chest over that simple, small gesture. They waited for me. I feel wanted here. Needed. These people are my family now, and I love them so very much. I am constantly reminding myself to never take this for granted—even the small things. I swallow a sip of wine, hoping to keep my emotions tucked away.

"Thank you," I murmur with a smile. "Where's Kase?"

"He's in the other room playing with the puppies and Ty's

dog," Margie tells me.

"Ty?" I ask, startled as she wanders off, not hearing me.

As in *hot Ty*? Hot mechanic Ty I've seen around but never been brave enough to speak to? Suddenly, I'm wishing I'd spent a little more time on my hair and maybe put on some mascara. Oh my God. Ty is *here*?

I head into the next room and freeze when I see a huge grey Pitbull staring at me with its tongue hanging out one side of its mouth, drool dripping onto my son who lies under it, giggling.

"Hi, Momma." Kase giggles. "Look at Nova. I love her." He wraps his feet around her, wrestling with her, and the dog leans into him and closes her eyes in utter bliss, clearly just as happy with him. Kase is always finding time to play with the dogs, he loves them so much.

"I see her," I say, hesitantly reaching over and scratching her ears. She's big, very stocky, and could easily be intimidating. Chip and Bossy, the black and white mutts that Evan rescued, are wrestling in the corner and tugging on a toy back and forth. About six months ago, Evan was out running when he found them abandoned in a trash bag. How anyone could ever do that is beyond me.

We had to leave our mini dachshund, Sassy, behind when we left Mississippi, and I miss her every day. Sometimes, in my mind's eye, I can see her propped up on the back of the couch, staring out the window, waiting for us to come home.

She's probably so sad and doesn't understand that I didn't have a choice.

Pitbulls sometimes get a bad rep, but judging by this dog's demeanor, she's more of a goofball than a threat. She leans in and closes her eyes again, seeming to enjoy the scratches from me.

"Good girl," I coo softly.

Our guests don't typically bring their pets to stay at the inn, but Evan doesn't discourage it. He loves animals and can't say no to anyone who asks. A while back, someone brought a cute ferret that liked to collect and hide things. He only stayed a short time, but he sure made life interesting when we found piles of random possessions it had hidden for weeks around the inn after he left.

Watching my son adjust over the past year has been such a relief. He smiles more, he doesn't jump at loud noises as much, and he's a lot more relaxed. We both are. I wonder, though, how much he remembers about our old life, about Sassy, even about his former name. He's never said anything, and I never bring it up.

Brianna and Jase became Mellie and Kase. I got Mellie from the show *Scandal,* one of my favorites back in the day, and Kase sounded like Jase. I wanted to give him a name that was easy to remember so he wouldn't slip up and tell anyone his real name. So far, it's working out.

We've had no issues so far, thankfully. When I'm around

guests or in town, I typically wear a hat and keep my head down, just to be safe. No one has ever seemed to recognize us, and the longer we're here, the more at ease I feel. Everyone here at the inn has just accepted us as is, without questioning us or forcing us to open up about our past. We created a basic story, and that's what we go with if we are asked. It's a relief to not be constantly fielding questions, to just be Mellie and Kase. The past is in the past.

"I see you met Nova," a deep, friendly voice drawls from behind me.

I startle and quickly lower my eyes, instinctively going into chameleon mode when I recognize that voice. I've seen Ty around town often, and I'm well aware of who he is, but he probably has no clue who I am given that we've only actually spoken one time. To say he's good looking is putting it mildly. He's like the ultimate manly-man cinnamon roll.

I've had a crush on him since the first time I laid eyes on him. It was last summer when we were both new here in town. I saw him fixing something at Sam's Auto Body when I walked by with Kase. He probably didn't even see me, but I couldn't have missed him, especially with his baseball hat on backward. I had no idea what he was fixing, but whatever it was, mine was broken. His intense blue eyes mirrored his dark blue coveralls, and the way he leaned over the engine with his biceps flexed still makes my heart go into overdrive when I think about it.

After that, I'd see him around town sporadically—at the local pizza place, the hardware store. And each time, I'd crush just a little bit harder. Then, I found out that it had been Beth's car he was fixing at the shop, and when he dropped it off at the inn last fall, I had been the only one there. I still remember taking the keys from him, the way my hand felt like it was on fire when I brushed his hand. Sure, he was friendly to me, but he didn't say much more than a handful of pleasantries. And I said nothing. I just continuously nodded like a yuppie and all but tripped over my own two feet.

Smooth, Mellie.

I still cringe at how awkward I was that day. God only knows what Ty must have thought of me.

I think every woman in Freedom Valley has at least a small crush on Ty, if the talk around town is to be believed. I mean, how could they not? His dark blond, neatly trimmed beard, his piercing blue eyes, and charisma that could charm anyone. He's got the blue-collar mechanic hotness going for him, but he also cleans up nice and looks smoking hot when I've seen him around in jeans and a flannel.

I'm a housekeeper at an inn, a single mom just trying to survive. He's way out of my league, anyway.

But to say my life is complicated is an understatement, and I have no time for getting involved with a man, no matter how hot. So, I'll just admire from afar and keep it moving.

"We haven't formally met," I say softly, coming back to the present, still stroking Nova's silky velvet head as she leans into my thigh. My gaze is still on the dog. I'm trying not to look at him because I'm afraid I'll spontaneously combust or forget my own name if I do.

"I'm Ty. And you're Mellie, right?" He squats down to pet Nova, who's now lying on her back, her feet in the air, accepting all the scratches and belly rubs with glee.

She reminds me of Sassy, who also loved belly rubs. Pain stabs me for a second, and I try to shake it off just like I do every time I remember something from before. Something that we had to leave behind. Most of it I can live without, but some things I do miss. Like my dog. I'd give anything to go back and get her. To some people they may say, it's just a dog, but to me, that dog is my family.

"Yes, and this is my son, Kase." I wave. *Ugh, why am I waving?* Keep it together, Mellie. *Keep it together.* I smooth my hoodie and stand. He's so handsome, it literally hurts my eyes to look at him, so I go back to petting the dog.

"It's nice to officially meet you both," he says with a tiny hint of a southern drawl that you might miss if you weren't listening for it. I actively try to hide my own drawl, so I'm aware of it when I hear it. Surrounded by all the New England accents, it's not hard to stand out if I'm not careful.

He speaks softly and slowly, almost as if he's trying to

hold it back. *Interesting*. I suppose it takes one to know one. I wonder if he can detect the accent that I'm trying hard to hide. Honestly, I have tried so hard to blend in and suppress it, and I think I've done a pretty good job of it.

What are *you* hiding, I wonder to myself as I sneak a glance to look him over.

Ty showed up in Freedom Valley around the same time that I did, and I don't know much about him. Come to think of it, I don't think anyone does. He reminds me a little bit of myself, like he's also sort of a chameleon.

I hate that I'm like this now. That I have to try and get reads on everyone to figure out if they're a potential threat or not. It's probably something I'll be doing for the rest of my life.

"Nice to finally meet you, as well," I say as I try not to stare, but he's making it hard. He continues to pet his dog, running his big hands over her head and ears.

And if all of this isn't bad enough, he also smells so good. Like pine, laundry soap, and something else I can't figure out. Maybe leather and motor oil. I catch myself staring at him, getting lost in his eyes, and quickly blink and look away. When I finally turn back, he's smiling, and he does not look away. *Nope.* He's smiling at me like he likes what he sees, and I'm starting to lose my senses. *Again.*

"You work here?" he asks, and something tells me he probably knows this already. Maybe he's just being friendly and I'm reading more into it.

I clear my throat. "I'm the inn housekeeper. What about you?"

He runs his hand over his beard and says, "I work nights over at Larkin as a mechanic, and I sometimes help Sam Sr. in his auto shop here in town."

"I remember you dropping Beth's car off a while back." I gaze at his trimmed beard and catch myself wanting to reach out and touch it. I wonder how old he is. He looks young with no grey in his beard or hair, and he has light wrinkles on the sides of his eyes when he smiles, so I'd guess early thirties. *Hot. Older man hot.*

Stop it. Ugh, I need to get out more. I've turned into the lonely lady creep here at the inn.

"Dinner!" Evan calls from the kitchen, interrupting us.

Thankful, I stand and say, "Well, it's nice to meet you both," as I give Nova one final scratch on her ears.

"You, as well. I hope to get to know you more." His gaze is warm on mine. The way he looks at me makes me nervous, but in a good way. Like he's interested in me, and that feels... strangely warm and fuzzy. If Evan invited him here, he must like him. Evan is former military, so nothing gets by him, which makes him outstanding at reading people and knowing who is good and who is not.

My stomach dips nervously and it's not because I'm afraid, which is my usual go-to. It's because I think we just had a moment right now. He had to have felt it too with the way he was looking at me.

"Let's go, buddy," I say softly to Kase, taking his little hand in mine.

"Nova, stay," Ty says as Nova's little nub of a tail wags so fast her whole body sways back and forth before she lies down and puts her head on her paws, keenly watching us.

"Wow. She'll just stay there, just like that?" I'm impressed at how calm and well-behaved she is.

"Yep. She won't go anywhere once I put her in place." He casually stands and tucks his hands into his front pockets, his blue eyes still focused on me. He's commanding, he's sexy, and he's making this room feel like a furnace all of a sudden. Jee-zuz.

Kase lets go of my hand and races to meet his friend Caleb in the dining room doorway, leaving me to walk down the hall next to Ty. I try to sneak another peek, noticing again how tall he is as he confidently walks in stride beside me. Not to mention that he seems at home here at the inn. I wonder why he's here for dinner, but knowing Evan, he probably ran into him in town and invited him, unofficial town mayor that he is.

As I step into the dining room, Allie hands me a plate and motions for me to get in line for the buffet. "Hey, girl! Can Kase sleep over with us tonight?" she asks. "Caleb got a new game he's dying to play with him. Some Pokémon thing.

Then tomorrow, Logan wanted to take them both out to play Pokémon Go."

"Sure. Sounds fun. That'll give me some time to get some more garden work in."

I'm supposed to have help getting my greenhouse put together, but the crew hasn't showed up—for three weeks in a row. They're probably not even coming. I just need to figure it out myself.

"You look lost in thought." Allie looks over at me.

"Sorry, just trying to figure out some things with my greenhouse plans."

"Ooohh, like what?"

Allie's brother Evan is who I would consider my best friend in Freedom Valley, but Allie and Beth have become my close friends, too. There's no mistaking her and Evan for siblings, they look so much alike, with dark hair and the brightest emerald green eyes. Allie's encouraged me with my gardening dreams, and sometimes she gets so excited for me that I forget that they're my dreams and not hers. I'm lucky to have a friend who has become like a sister to me, especially one who our sons have become inseparable too, acting like best friends almost immediately.

"I've been trying to get my greenhouse together so I can do more seed startings. I just got more seeds in, and I'm excited to get them going. I was counting on the greenhouse space. I need to get everything growing now so that I have plenty to sell at the farmers' market all summer and fall."

I work on my garden plans when I'm not doing my housekeeping duties, so my time is very limited. Not having the greenhouse finished has set me back, but I don't want to tell her that. It's my problem, not theirs. Allie, Evan, and everyone else at the inn have their own stuff going on.

The farmers' market started as a result of me wanting to give back to the community here in Freedom Valley and bring positive attention to the inn. This past year was a rough time for the inn, and Evan almost lost it due to the bank threatening to foreclose. But we brought back the fall festival tradition and made enough money to turn the inn around and save it. Without Beth's help with all of that, I don't know if we'd still be here right now. We're trying to integrate the inn into the community as much as we can. There's a spot on the back of the property where we host the fall festival that I dreamed of using for a farmers' market. I thought it would be a good way to bring in more vendors, customers, and the community. It's been coming together, and I can't wait to host the first one as soon as everything is ready.

"I can't wait to see your farmers' market come together. Oh, and before I forget, I baked you a loaf of sourdough with roasted garlic and rosemary from your garden herbs. It's still warm." Allie motions to her purse sitting on a chair in the corner of the room, a foil wrapped package next to it.

"Thank you." My mouth waters at the thought of her bread. "I'll never turn down your sourdough. It's the best."

Allie's baking is on another level. I've never tasted such delicious breads and pastries, and her passion for baking is like mine for gardening. Watching her do what she loves every day has inspired me and given me permission to pursue what I love. Allie's success isn't surprising, though, because she is one of the most persistent people I know. She began her bakery business out of the kitchen here at the inn and has now been able to open a new location here in town called Baked Inn Love—another extension and nod to the Golden Gable Inn that's been in her family for generations. She's planning on moving the business there within the next few weeks.

We move up in the line and I make plates for both Kase and me. By the time I get Kase set up next to Caleb at the kids' table, there's only one seat left at the big table. Right next to Ty.

Great.

I'm nervous as I move toward him, but a small part of me is excited. I want to have grown-up conversations and make friends. *Friends*, I tell myself. It's okay to have friends. Nothing more.

I remind myself that he's just a guest here, having dinner like the rest of us. I slide in next to him with a small, hesitant smile, and he smiles back but continues talking to Logan.

Even so, his body shifts to the side to include me in his conversation at the table and I feel a little bit giddy that he wants me to sit there. I catch him look over every so often and smile when he catches my eye. I can't even help it. Ugh. I'm ridiculous. What is this, high school?

Logan leans forward to get my attention through the buzz of noise at the table. "I picked up some of that deer netting you were asking about that we can put around the garden area. I left it in the barn for whenever you need it."

"Thanks, that's going to help so much. There's always a ton of deer back there and I can't have them eating up all my vegetables."

"It's a hundred-foot roll, so that should do it. It's heavy, so when you're ready, Pete or I can help you get it set up." He forks a bite of his pasta and sits back in his chair as he shoves it into his mouth. "This is so good."

"Yeah, it really is good," I say, looking over to Sasha and smiling. "Thanks for dinner, Sash."

Sasha beams at us from across the table. "My pleasure, love. When are you going to be bringing me my bountiful produce to cook with?"

"Hopefully here in a few weeks you'll have more produce than you'll know what to do with. Forget the grocery store. I'll have you covered with organic fresh-grown goods right from my own two hands."

I accidentally graze Ty's hand with mine as we both reach

for a piece of garlic bread. My hand zings where it touched his and my heart flutters with unexpected excitement. Ty seems unfazed by the contact and casually asks, "So, how did you get into gardening?"

Now my heart races with panic. The truth is right on the tip of my tongue, but not something I feel comfortable sharing. I swallow and finally pull it together enough to reply with not the whole truth but at least part of it.

"I started playing around with the herb garden last year and I really enjoyed it. So, this year I decided to take a part of the back property that already had a few garden plots cleared and turn them into full gardens. I'm growing vegetables for the inn and starting my own locally grown farmers' market. You know, something to bring the Freedom Valley community together."

He nods. "That's really cool. My momma gardened a lot, I used to love helping her."

"Your momma sounds like a good southern woman," I hedge, hoping I'm right in my accent assessment.

He pauses, then gives me the side eye and says with a chuckle, "Who says she's southern?"

"Isn't she?" I ask, playing it cool. "Pretty sure I'm detecting a hint of a southern accent." Now I give him the side eye with a smile.

"I guess it takes one to know one," he says with a sly grin.

My heart is pounding in my chest with panic washing over

me. *Shit. Shit. Shit.*

I quickly recover and say, "Why do you say that?"

"Darlin', you sound about as southern as I do." He relaxes when he says this, and his southern drawl is now full-on, like he's not even trying to hold it back.

His eyes lock on mine, and we stare at each other for a minute, like this is a duel. Finally, he says softly, "Alabama."

And I whisper, "Mississippi."

"Howdy, neighbor," he says, breaking out of our stare down and taking another bite of his food like it's no big deal, his eyes still flicking back to me in a way that makes me feel comforted instead of fearful. Nothing about Ty screams scary or alarming. Something about how he carries himself is just... calming and peaceful. He's like a big teddy bear. I bet he gives really good hugs.

It may not be a big deal for him, but I can't believe I just freely admitted that to him. I have no idea why I even did that, and I feel my ears begin to burn with regret and worry.

"I don't talk about home too much. This is home now," I start rambling, trying to steer him back to Freedom Valley.

"Same," he says. "I like it here." He focuses on me when he says that, and he doesn't look away for quite a while. When he finally does, he flashes me that panty-dropping grin again.

As bowls of sourdough garlic bread are passed around, I grab another piece and take a bite of the buttery, rosemary goodness. I close my eyes and try not to moan, it's so good.

I glance at Allie, who's watching me with a smirk on her face. She's enjoying watching me squirm next to Ty and I know she's going to tease me about it later with Beth. I feel my face get hot and I focus on my bread. "Great bread, Allie. How's the bakery coming along?"

"Good. I'll be glad when it finally moves out of my kitchen and officially into the new building in town."

"I got you covered with fresh herbs," I offer.

"I'm counting on that. Fresh is always the best. My sourdough loaves with fresh herbs always go fast."

"Because they're so good, Ace," Logan says as he leans over and kisses her on the cheek.

She smiles warmly. "Thanks, babe."

We enjoy our meal and conversation. Every so often, loud laughter breaks out, and before we know it, we find ourselves still chatting long past when everyone has finished eating—plates pushed back, utensils abandoned, some making room for seconds, nobody feeling lonely or hungry.

Whenever I leave one of these big family dinners at the inn, my heart is happy and my cup is full. It's like my soul has been recharged.

As Ty gets up to get more food, Logan beams, "Hey, look who's here!" He's looking beyond me, toward the doorway. "Preston, my man. There's still plenty of food left. Grab a plate."

"Sorry I'm late. Traffic coming up from Boston was a nightmare." Preston waves at everyone as he heads to the stack of plates at the buffet table.

"Glad you made it," Evan says, standing to shake his hand. "How long you here for?"

"About a week. Do you have space available?"

"No problem at all." Evan claps him on the back. "Get yourself some dinner and let's catch up. Beer?"

"Sure," Preston replies.

Preston and I have always had a strong friendship, but I think he may like me in a different way than I like him. "Hey, Mel. Save me a spot, will you?" he asks, gesturing to Ty's empty seat.

I watch Ty slide back into his seat, setting his plate full of seconds on the table. He turns to me, a satisfied smile on his face knowing there isn't a spot for Preston now. I give Preston an apologetic smile with a shrug before refocusing on Ty next to me.

He did that on purpose, I'm sure of it. What in the world?

~

CHAPTER 2

Mellie

Butterflies be damned.
I like that man.

It's late when I get back to my room after dinner. I'm curled up on my couch with a steaming mug of tea and the new Bakers Heirloom Seed catalog. It's full of amazing, colorful vegetables that I can't wait to try my hand at growing. I know I'll probably need to keep it simple this year and start with a few things, then add on next year. This year is my practice garden, my time to experiment, trial and error, figuring out what grows best where, what needs more sun, different amendments in the soil. If I mess up, I mess up, but nothing will keep me from dreaming up cool plans for future gardens.

I have big dreams. I may even go full-on farmer and add some chickens, maybe some goats for fresh milk and cheese. My hobby has quickly turned into a new job that I'm lucky Evan and Beth encourage me to pursue. They both see my vision for this and want it to be a success, not just for the inn but for my happiness.

I imagine the possibility of making my own cheeses from goat milk, growing over half of the food for the inn, and raising farm-fresh eggs. Being able to create our own food is magical.

A knock at my door startles me and makes my heart clench for a moment. I wonder if I'll ever truly shake the feeling of looking over my shoulder—hopefully someday. I know I will probably always be on edge in some ways, but it has gotten a little easier to relax, especially here at the inn. It helps that we got far away, but some days, it still doesn't seem far enough.

I unlock the door to find Preston holding two plates and I motion for him to come in.

"I come bearing dessert," he says. "I saw you didn't have any. So, when I got seconds, I thought I'd bring you firsts."

Preston has been a good friend to me and everyone else here at the inn. He's like a walking hug. He's my friend and I'm thankful for him, and as much as I wish I had feelings for him, they're just not there. I haven't been able to imagine finding a new partner anyway. He's also been good for me, helping me remember that not all men are scary and bad. He's one of the few people I've allowed myself to open up to.

"That does sound good. Come on in. Do you want some tea?" I head to the tiny kitchen and turn the kettle back on.

He hesitates then says, "I'm not much of a tea guy, but sure." He sets down the plates on my coffee table and looks around, taking in my small space.

"I've never been up here. I didn't imagine it would look like this."

"Like what?"

"It's beautiful, like out of a magazine. Did you do all this yourself?" He runs his hand over the quilt on the back of the couch.

"I did," I say as I wait for the water to boil. "Mostly thrifting and DIY projects. I like to make things."

"I could see that downstairs when I first walked in and saw your... collection. What are you growing?" His eyes roam around the plants I have set up.

"Tomatoes, cucumbers, peppers, kale, lettuce, beets, cauliflower, zucchini, and squash. You have to start some of the seeds inside under a grow light during the cold months. Then you plant them outside when it's safe, after the last frost for our zone." I realize I'm excited-rambling. "Sorry, I get excited about it all and everyone around here is probably tired of hearing me talk about dirt and seeds." I grin at him.

"That makes sense. So they're only in here temporarily then," he says, looking relieved at the jungle in my loft. "You're really into this."

I pour water over the tea bag in his mug and set it down on a coaster in front of him.

"Gardening has been such a good outlet for me. There's just something about having my hands in the dirt. It's kind of like new beginnings."

Preston knows a little about my past and how Kase and I got to the inn. Evan and I told him some of the story last fall just to make sure we were being careful. I would never want anyone here to be put in jeopardy over helping me. Preston is like the protective older brother to everyone here, and I have no reason not to fully trust him.

He pushes my tiramisu closer to me and picks up his plate. "You really light up when you talk about your gardening. You deserve to harvest great things."

I know Preston had feelings for me when we first met, but I just didn't feel the same. I know he has to feel that, too, because there's just no chemistry between us like that. It's like Evan and me. We rib each other and are like family. This is why I think there's something wrong with me, like I'm damaged. I'm meant to be an old lady who drinks tea and gardens. This is it for me at twenty-six. I'm meant to raise my son and be alone, and I think I'm okay with that.

"Thanks. It feels good to have a purpose and something to get out of bed for that is exciting every day. Anyway, enough about me. What about you? How's it going getting moved up here from Boston?"

"It's slow," he admits, then takes a bite of his tiramisu. "I'm grateful to be able to stay here while I make the transition."

"Why so slow?" I ask, then take a sip of my tea.

"I need to find an office assistant, and I need help getting my new practice up and going. Know anyone who would be interested in a job?"

I think back to when I first met Bradley. I was the office manager at a dental office, helping with all the billing and staffing. I loved that job, and they were good to me there. I even brought Kase to work with me for a while when I came off maternity leave, letting him sleep in his bouncy chair while I worked. I couldn't leave him at home because of Bradley's temper, and eventually, things got so tense at home that I had to quit my job.

I consider Preston's offer. Opening up the can of worms of my past could potentially give up our location and safety. I love our life now. Sure, cleaning rooms isn't glamorous, but I'm happy. This past year has been healing for me, being able to create new routines, and I love working with everyone here. Plus, Kase is always nearby so I know he's safe, and that's what matters the most.

Preston helped Evan save the inn last year when the bank was trying to take it, and he helped Allie in her custody fight with her ex. He has been good to everyone here, and I'd help him out if I could.

"Off the top of my head, no."

"Well, if you do hear of anyone, let me know. I really could use the help making this transition go smoother."

"I sure will." I take another bite.

He presses again, "Have you decided to take me up on my offer of helping you figure out your legal stuff with your ex?"

I know I need to face my past and find a way to get a divorce so that I can become truly free. The thought of doing that and facing Bradley again is just terrifying and exhausting. It's taken me a year to learn to relax and heal as best I can, and I still feel like I have a long way to go. I don't regret leaving like we did, but now I have to make sure there aren't any legal ramifications. Eventually I will have to face that.

"I would love that, but I can't afford you, Pres."

"Who said anything about paying me?"

I tilt my head at him. "You can't help everyone for free. You have a business to run."

"It's called pro-bono. And I have plenty of work lined up with paying clients, too. There's a need for my law practice up here."

"I'm glad you're here."

"So let me help you."

"With the gardening? Sure," I tease as I hold up the catalogue.

"If that's what you need." He shrugs.

I laugh. "When is the last time you got your hands dirty?" I ask, looking at his white sweater, crisp jeans, and buttery brown leather shoes.

He cocks his head for a minute, I guess thinking things through. "Never," he finally admits, laughing. "But I thought I'd throw the offer out there."

I take a bite of cake and mull it over. There's no denying it would be nice to finally and legitimately put everything behind me, especially with how stressful it is being on the run.

"What would that look like?"

"Whatever you want it to. We can figure out how to file for divorce, file charges, whatever you want. Legally, this is a shit show, Mel. You know that. We have to do the right thing and make sure you and Kase are protected at all costs."

"You promise you'll keep us safe?"

"Between all of us here, we'll always do what's best for *you*, Mel. You're my friend." He smiles sadly.

Preston is a total catch. He's tall, with short, dark hair and whiskey-colored eyes. He's like the good-looking, boy-next-door type of guy. When he smiles, he has dimples so deep you could swim in them. On paper, he's the perfect man and more. Some lady will be very lucky to have him.

But then I think about the way Ty makes my belly flip flop every time I see him and having him in very close proximity tonight reminded me of that feeling.

I try to shake away these thoughts, needing to focus on what's in front of me.

"We're all going to McGuiness Tavern tomorrow night. Want to come?"

I take another bite of my cake and look at him as he's waiting for my answer. "I don't know."

"That new guy you were sitting with, Ty? He's coming..."

Well, crap on a cracker. That makes it easier. "Yeah, I guess I can do that. I haven't been out in a while."

"They're playing matchmaker again," he warns. "They said there's a barista from the coffee shop they want me to meet, and you're on the books for Ty."

I laugh. "You know that's what they do. You're a catch, Preston. You deserve to find a nice lady."

He tilts his head at me and gives a half smile. "And you deserve to find a man who treats you the right way."

I sigh. "I don't know, Pres. I'm still legally married, and I'm just so tired from all that. I don't know if I'll ever be able to put myself out there again."

"All in time, Mellie," he muses, looking at my catalogue, open to a page with bright photos of thyme on it. "Like thyme, the herb, all in thyme."

I chuckle. "You're a dork. But we can be each other's wingmen, like Goose and Maverick. I'll help you find your new lady."

His brows come together, but he grins. "I'm *not* Goose. I'm Maverick."

"Fine, I'll be your Goose." I shrug my shoulders and take a sip of my tea.

"Well, I've got to go settle in for the night. Thanks for the tea." He gathers up our dishes to take back with him.

"You're welcome. Thanks for the dessert and the company, Maverick," I tease as I walk him to the door.

He leans in and kisses my cheek. "See you later, Goose."

As he heads down the stairs, I shut the door and lock it behind him, thinking back on the night. Thinking of Preston, and Ty, and relationships.

I used to want a guy that is like the ultimate cinnamon roll in the romance books I listen to when I work. A guy who gives me butterflies, even though I think those only happen in books and movies. The only thing I've ever felt is my stomach being tied up in knots.

But when I fall asleep that night, I dream of Ty, and I like it. Butterflies be damned, I think I like that man.

CHAPTER 3

Ty

Complicated doesn't scare me.

I pull up to McGuinness Tavern and put my truck in park, pulling my ballcap down. I haven't been out in a while, and when Evan and his crew asked me to come hang out tonight, I almost said no.

But then they mentioned she'd be here, too, and I couldn't pass that up. I've wanted to talk to Mellie for months, I just haven't had the chance. Seeing her at dinner turned me into a nervous teenage boy with sweaty palms. Why does this woman make me so nervous? To say she's beautiful would be an understatement. She's stunning, but she's got something mysterious about her, like she has layers. Layers I'm curious to discover and understand.

I've been seeing her around for a while now. She's tiny, only coming up to my chest, and I'm a good six feet. She carries herself like she's invisible, but she couldn't be invisible if she tried. Her shiny blond hair, striking light green eyes, and those adorable freckles speckled across her nose and cheeks. I couldn't stop watching her, and the little glances she sent my way every so often didn't go unnoticed.

She's just cool, and I even like her kid. I've always liked kids, though, and desperately want some of my own. The fact that I'm thirty-one and don't have any yet is a disappointment both to me and to my momma.

As I slide out of my truck, I notice a row of motorcycles lined up at the front of the tavern. I recognize Toad, a member of the local motorcycle club, who waves to me. These guys all bring their bikes into Sam's shop regularly to get worked on, and I've made friends with several of them. They're mostly good guys who do a lot for the community. I've heard a few of them may be sketchy, but Toad is good people.

"Flynn." Toad nods in my direction.

"What's up, man?" I call as I round the steps to the tavern.

"Biking and working. The usual. See you inside?"

I wave as I head into the tavern where the delicious aroma of pub food and good music hits me right away. Walking into the McGuiness Tavern is like coming home to your momma's for supper, only there's a live band and lots of people buzzing about. Freedom Valley isn't really the kind of town you can get lost in. Everyone knows everyone, and they look out for each other here. A generous share of tourists come through, but McGuiness is purely a spot for the locals to catch up on everybody's business. As a newer resident in town, I love listening to the comings and goings of what's going on.

I spot them in the corner as Beth and Mellie pull up chairs to a big round wooden table. I nab a seat next to Mellie. She looks surprised and stills for a second, then smiles shyly at me.

"Hi," she says softly, then glances over at Beth and Allie. I don't miss the shit-eating grins Allie and Beth shoot back at her. It appears I have her friends' approval, and that might go a long way toward winning hers.

"Glad you could make it out," Logan says as our server makes her rounds and takes his drink order.

"Evan's playing the next few songs, then he'll come grab a bite with us," Beth says, waving at Evan up on stage.

As the music plays, Mellie sneaks a few glances my way. Every time she does, I smile at her, and every time I do, she looks like she doesn't know what to do with herself. She's cute as pie, and I want a taste. I've waited months to get to know her, and now is my time to shoot my shot.

"It feels good to get out of the house tonight. Not have

to think about how much work we still need to do and just catch up with you guys," Allie says. She then turns her attention to Preston. "Speaking of catching up, when are you officially moved up here for good?"

I watch him, trying to figure out his interest with Mellie. He's sitting next to her, but his body language isn't showing me he's into her like that, and she sure as shit isn't sneaking glances at him the way she is with me tonight.

Logan sits with his arm draped over Allie's shoulders and she leans in every now and then to whisper something to him and smiles. Now *they* are a couple. Preston and Mellie don't look like they're a thing. This is my chance to make her *my* thing.

"I still have a few weeks to wrap up in Boston, and then I'll be up here full-time from then on."

"When you need a hand, just let me know," Logan responds, tipping his beer bottle up at Preston and taking a swig.

See, this is one of my favorite things about this town. They are like family, always offering to help each other out, and they pulled me into their circle without a second thought. This is the type of place I want to call home and put down roots of my own, start my own family.

"Will do." Preston looks over at me and it feels like he's trying to get a read on me, as well. Nothing about his stance is showing me he's bothered by me being here. Maybe this will be easier than I thought. I thought this might be a friendly competitive thing, but it's possible they're just friends. Hopefully that's the case. I don't need to be on anyone's radar or step on any toes right now—or ever—but I'm not afraid to go for what I want, and what I want is to know Mellie more.

My gaze drifts over to Mellie, finding her eyes already on me. "Want to dance?" I ask her impulsively.

Everyone goes quiet at the table, and I can see her wanting to decline. I reach over and take her hand. "Just one?" I stare into her eyes and give her a big smile that I know she won't be able to resist.

Preston eyes us curiously but doesn't say anything as he takes a sip of his drink. Yep. Just as I thought, friend zone for these two. Thank fuck.

I guide her onto the dance floor, her hand still in mine. I don't let go, I just pull her in closer and hold her hand softly in mine.

"I'm not a very good dancer," she admits nervously.

"Me neither, darlin'. Let's just pretend we know how." I chuckle as I lead her, my hand in hers.

"What made you want to dance with me if you don't dance?" She leans into me a little and I feel her relax slightly.

"I want to get to know you more," I say softly.

She lets out a nervous laugh. She's an enigma. She's beautiful, yet she carries herself like she doesn't even know it. She's wearing a black crocheted tank top that shows off her toned arms and shoulders and a long, patterned skirt with a slit up the side, revealing a strong, tanned leg. I'd like to explore that leg with my hand, but of course, I refrain. At least for now. But damn, she's gorgeous as all get out. Holding her on the dance floor, my hand grazing the bare skin on her back, this is the hardest dance I've ever done, and I mean in more ways than one.

She glances up at me. "Well now that we're out here, you seem like you really do know how to dance." Her eyes meet mine. "And I'm also not very good with new people." This feels like a silent warning.

"Me neither. I guess we both have our struggles." I shrug like it's no big deal.

"What kind of struggles do you have?" She tilts her head up at me.

My eyes drag over her adorable freckles again, her face a little flushed, probably with nervousness, and her green eyes lock on mine. "Not really any struggles. I just know what it's like to be new in town, to be lonely."

"Are you lonely, Ty?" She rests her palms flat on my shoulders as we move to the music.

"Not anymore." I break into a wide smile.

"You're such a flirt." She laughs, and I can feel her starting to relax even more as she leans into me, probably partly to hear me over the loud music.

"Only with you," I admit.

"Are you seeing anyone? Single?" she asks, biting her lip like she's going to be devastated if I say I am.

"Wouldn't be dancing with you if I was seeing someone, darlin'."

She looks relieved and nods. "Good."

"I wouldn't mind seeing you around a lot more, though," I hedge as the song picks up a bit. My guard is down with Mellie, my southern accent not clipped back at all at this point. I'm on a high, dancing this close to her. Feeling her in my arms, looking into her eyes, and letting go, I almost forget who I am and why I'm here in Freedom Valley in the first place.

Her eyes tip up to mine. "New Hampshire is a long way away from Alabama. You plan on sticking around?"

And this is where it gets tricky for me. I don't want to lie to her, but I can't exactly tell her the truth of why I'm here, so I deflect her question as much as I can.

"As is Mississippi," I hedge. Her eyes flash something I can't fully detect, but it's not something good, and she tenses up a bit. This makes me back off a little and want to lighten the mood.

Before I can get a word in, she asks, "What brings you here?" She's good, once again bringing the focus back onto me.

"Work and a fresh start, if we're being honest."

"Same," she says, looking like she's lost in thought.

"How come we haven't hung out much until now?"

"I didn't realize you even knew who I was."

"I've definitely seen you around, but you always seemed busy and I never got the chance to say hello. Didn't feel right then," I say. Whatever distance and nerves we had at the beginning of this song are close to gone as we dance, our bodies practically molded together. I can't take my eyes off her lips, and I wonder what it would be like to kiss her. I catch her staring at mine too, as if she's thinking the same thing.

"I've been busy. Between my son, work, and the gardens, I haven't had a lot of time to make friends outside of the inn."

The music picks up again, and I lean in, whispering into her ear, "I'm glad you weren't too busy to be here tonight."

"Me too," she says, her eyes on my mouth again. I pull her closer, but she lays her head on my chest during a slow song. It seems like we've been dancing forever, and I don't want to stop.

"Would you want to go out sometime?" I ask boldly.

She looks like she wants to say yes, but instead she says, "I want to, but my life is about to get even busier." Something tells me this isn't the reason, more that she's scared or nervous to start something new. I'm terrified myself, but damn if I don't want to explore this chemistry with her. She feels intoxicating to be with, in the best way possible.

"Well," I shrug, "I guess I'll just have to help you garden," I say as I spin her around. Now her back is pressed up against me and she throws her head back and laughs. And just as I suspected, she has a beautiful laugh, too. Everything I'm seeing about Mellie so far is just pulling me in. She's a damn dream.

"You did say you have gardening experience. I don't know... You could be useful." She folds her hands around the back of my neck, and for a minute, I picture us not here on this dance floor but somewhere where it's just us.

"I can be *very* useful," I flirt, pulling her closer to me as a slow song begins to play. I've lost track of how many songs we've danced to, forgotten about ordering dinner or our friends probably watching us from the table. I know nothing except for this woman and this woman only.

Her eyes lock on mine, and for a second, I almost lean in and kiss her, but I don't want to rush things with her. I want to get to know her more. She's quiet, mysterious, and perceptive. I want her to let me into her busy world. Whatever I have to do to get to know her more, I'll take my time and make sure I do it right.

Mellie leans even farther into me as we dance. It feels good to hold her, and I don't want the song to end.

She pulls back a little and says, "Thanks, Ty."

"For what?"

"For being kind to me. You seem like a nice guy."

I push a piece of her long hair back from her face and tuck it behind her ear and kiss her cheek. "I try to be a nice guy."

"I don't trust people very easily," she whispers into my ear.

I nod, realizing I'd read her nerves right. "It's okay. Not everyone should be trusted. You should make people earn it. How can I earn *your* trust?" I tow her off the dance floor and tuck her into a quiet corner of the bar, just out of sight of our friends.

She murmurs into my ear above the loud music, "I don't know. But you seem to be doing just fine so far."

"Oh, yeah?" I grin down at her, my eyes on her mouth that is looking mighty kissable right about now. All my holding back is about to go out the window.

"Are you going to kiss me or what?" Her lip turns up in a small smirk.

"You want me to?" I ask, surprised by her boldness.

"Yeah," she says softly, tilting her head up.

I pull her into me, my lips hitting her soft ones. She leans in and kisses me back firmly, passionately, and her arms wrap around my back and travel up to my neck.

My hands cup her face and I pull her in closer and kiss her until I feel like I've lost my mind a bit. She smells amazing, a mixture of vanilla and coconut, and I like it. Kissing her is like lying in the sand on a warm beach, drinking an iced-cold beer.

We finally pull out of the kiss, slow at first, like magnets trying to disconnect.

"Wow," she breathes.

"Wow," I say back like an idiot.

"I'm complicated, Ty."

"Good."

"How is that good?"

"Complicated doesn't scare me." I kiss her again until I about forget my own name, and the way she kisses me back, I have a feeling she's forgotten hers, too. All I know is that I don't want to stop kissing this woman.

CHAPTER 4

～

Mellie

I want things I can't have with him.

Rain taps against the roof of the garden shed as Evan steps inside and wipes his boots on the mat.

"What's all this?" He looks around, amused at the jungle I've created in the laundry room.

While my plants everywhere make sense to me, I realize to others it looks like something someone would make a meme out of. The crisp, pungent smell of tomato vines and fragrant herbs permeates the air. The plants have been getting big. It's crazy how fast they grow under the lights, and it makes me even more excited to see how they thrive when I get them in the ground.

I remember when I told Bradley about my interest in gardening books and magazines. He hated any time I found something that made me happy, when the focus wasn't fully on him, and his reactions were enough to deter me from bringing it up. I began to hide my interest in gardening, and I never planted anything in my old home. My old life.

As Evan wanders down the rows of starter plants, I start to feel nervous he may think I've gone overboard and be upset about the mess. I know he won't react like Bradley did, but I still don't want him upset at anything I did.

"I'm sorry..." I stammer. My heart races and my stomach drops, panic engulfing me. "I can find somewhere else—" I freeze as I stand at a table full of spray bottles to replenish my cleaning cart.

He turns to face me. "No. This is incredible, Mel. There's... just so many. I'm seriously impressed." He scratches his beard and looks around some more. "What do the different colors mean?" he asks, trying to decipher the map I drew indicating the different colored popsicle sticks I use to mark each variety.

I let out a breath I didn't realize I'd been holding. "These are different varieties of heirloom seeds. I bartered mostly for them in local garden groups," I tell him proudly. "We have several kinds of all of the plants, actually."

Evan scratches the back of his head and says, "You have

quite literally outgrown the garden shed," he says. "Beth told me this was amazing, so I had to see it for myself."

I laugh at his pun. "I'm trying to use my space wisely."

"Yeah, but these are only going to get bigger. You need more space."

I do need more space. Luckily, I'm just starting the seeds and getting them ready to be planted outside when it's warm enough. When I have the greenhouse up and going, that will help tremendously.

"I'm just grateful to have a place to stay," I say quietly. "You've done so much for us, Evan."

"Well, you've done so much for the inn, Mellie. Having you and Kase here has been great. I never have to worry about anything with the housekeeping. You go above and beyond. That takes a lot of stress off everyone. What you do here really matters, and we're so grateful for you."

"Thanks," I say, ducking my head down to hide my face. I'm not much of a crier, but my love and gratitude for Evan has always run deep. He'll never know how much he means to me and Kase.

If it wasn't for my neighbor across the street from our old house, Mitch, we'd never be here at the inn. Mitch saw things that worried him—rightfully so—and did something about it. The first time Mitch contacted me was when Bradley and I were in the front yard watching Kase ride his scooter. Bradley was enraged that I was wearing shorts outside and accused me of trying to get Mitch's attention with my bare legs. He knocked me down and kneeled over me, screaming with his fist ready, and when he saw Mitch watching, he pretended to hug me and whispered in my ear bitterly, "You better act right, whore."

After that, Mitch made secretive yet bold moves to check in on me and Kase, letting it be known that when we needed his help, he'd be there. And when the day came that we did need him, he got us out and took us to his Marine buddy Evan Harper. And this life we live now, here with Evan and this found family, is something I'll never take for granted.

He looks around. "Where's Kase?"

"He's upstairs with Caleb, watching a movie."

I'm so grateful Kase has Caleb. I've felt so guilty about the way we've had to hide out and change everything about ourselves and our lives. Kase has been a good sport about it all, but I know that things have been hard for my little man. We've both been healing and finding a new normal here, but we're both happier by leaps and bounds.

The boys alternate between hanging out here at our loft and at Allie and Logan's neighboring farmhouse, which is just a short ATV ride away. I picked up an older ATV with two booster seats in the back, making it easier to get the boys back and forth and to get around the grounds.

"Maybe it's time to think about something bigger for you guys." Evan stuffs his hands in his pockets.

"What did you have in mind? You want us to find a place in town?" I start to feel panic creep in. I don't have enough money saved up to get my own place yet or proper identification to rent anything. Does Evan want us to move? Where will we go?

As if sensing my panic, Evan holds his hand up. "No, that's not what I meant. Do you know the bunkhouse by the pole barn, between here and Logan and Allie's property?"

"The one out by the gardens?"

"Yes. Maybe you and Kase could think about moving out there. You could be closer to the gardens and use the pole barn and have more room for your... jungle."

I snort. "It's not a jungle, Evan. And hopefully my greenhouse will be finished soon so I can move things into there, as well."

"Oh, it's a jungle. Do you know how tall some tomato plants can get?" he deadpans.

I grit my teeth and shake my head. "I mean... no. I'm learning everything via YouTube and Google."

"Yeah, well, some of them get pretty big. And you have... what, over ninety tomato plants? Do you realize how much space ninety tomato plants will take up?"

I cover my mouth. *Oof.* To be honest, I didn't think about that. Holy crap. And the tomatoes are just some of the starters. I have cucumbers, various herbs, and other plants strategically taking up every bit of precious real estate out here in the garden shed. And honestly? I wish I could do even more. This is kind of amazing. It's the coolest thing I've ever done, other than become a mom.

"Why don't you head out to the bunkhouse tomorrow and take a look, see what you think."

I think this is a great idea already. When we first got here, I felt safe being close to everyone, centrally located here in the loft of the shed. But now that we've been here a while and are settled in, I'm feeling braver. I could make the bunkhouse work. Evan's just a short distance away.

"I wouldn't mind having a little more room to grow." I can't help but smile at the thought of that.

"This makes you happy, and it's good to finally see you happy, Mel."

I punch him softly in the arm. "Don't make me get all sappy, Evan."

"You're doing great. Seriously. I'm proud of you. Beth is excited for you, too."

I take a deep breath and realize I am happy. For the first time in a very long time, it just feels so good to finally be content. It's been a hell of a year. Things are looking up, and we're in a good place. There's so much to be grateful for.

"Thanks, Ev. For everything."

"Alright, buddy, put your shoes on so we can go see the bunkhouse," I tell Kase, and he quickly scrambles, as excited as I am to explore our new potential home.

"What's it like?" he asks eagerly.

"I don't know. I've never been inside. We'll get to see it for the first time together."

"Can I have my own room?"

"Probably."

"Can I bring my toys?" he asks. We had to leave everything behind and start over once already, and I'm sure he's worried we'll have to do that again. I want to reassure him that this isn't like when we had to up and run suddenly.

"Of course. And you'll be closer to Caleb's house so you guys can play more. He can come to our new house, too."

"Yes!" he says excitedly. "Okay, I'm ready. Let's go, Momma."

"Hold onto the railing," I call as we head down the stairs.

I buckle Kase in and slide into my seat. We ride slowly, taking in the new colorful buds starting to pop in on the trees. Everything is starting to bloom. I can't wait to see how the gardens will look. I've planted so many bulbs and seeds around with the help of Pete, our handyman. It's so exciting to see everything come vibrantly to life. The inn has truly transformed even more into a luxurious property that has beauty in every corner. Being in this environment never gets old. If I could camp out here, I probably would. I love being outside, planting something new or thinking of something to landscape. Pete loves it too, so I can usually dream up a vision and he'll help me make it come to life.

We pull up to the bunkhouse to find a truck I don't recognize out front. Evan didn't mention that anyone would be working on it today. "Stay here, buddy. Let me go check first."

I walk over to the truck and look in. There's a Snap On Tools ball cap on the middle armrest and the back is full of tools and a large toolbox. I head to the bunkhouse and knock. A dog barks, making me jump. I knock again, a little harder this time, which makes the dog yap even louder. Maybe Logan had someone come out and do some work to get the bunkhouse ready for us?

I peer inside. A grey Pitbull lunges against the window, still barking, making me jump and almost fall off the small front porch.

Is that...? No. It can't be.

Just then, the front door jerks open, and Ty stands there shirtless with black sweatpants hung low on his waist. His hair is messy, like he just woke up. He blinks and steps back, confused when he sees me. "Mellie. What are you doing here?"

"What are *you* doing here?" I ask, just as confused.

"I live here," he says slowly. Nova yips in recognition of me, her tail wagging now that she's deemed there's no official threat. He bensd down and lays his hand on her head. The dog looks at him sideways.

"Since when? Evan said we could stay here and use the pole barn. He didn't mention anyone else living here."

He just stares at me sleepily, like he's trying to wake up or figure out what to say or both. "Logan rented it to me a week ago."

Ugh. I groan and cover my eyes. "How am I going to explain this to Kase?"

He runs a hand over his jaw. "I'm sorry, Mellie. I didn't know."

I look back at Kase's hopeful face then back at Ty, standing there looking like a delicious snack, and I feel like I don't know which way to turn. Go back to my ATV and disappoint my son? Or stay here and converse with the hottest man alive who just rolled out of bed who I very much would like to roll back into bed with if the circumstances were very different?

Focus, I remind myself. Okay, the garden shed will be fine. We'll be fine. It just sucks that we couldn't be out here closer to the gardens.

"It's good to see you again," he says softly. He looks unsure what else to say and this just got even more awkward. How can we go from glued to each other and kissing the other night to this?

I just stare at him. I don't even know what to think. I'm

upset about the bunkhouse, and he has the nerve to stand there without a shirt on, showing off these sexy tattoos that snake up and down his upper body. And his messy bedhead is seriously messing with my lady parts right now. I want to kiss him again, but I also want to kick him in the shins for taking the bunkhouse. Ugh. I'm mad, both at myself and at the circumstances that I know are not his fault, yet here we are.

He crosses his arms and leans against the doorway, watching me, sensing my agitation. He says nothing. Nova sits next to him, panting, her wild tongue hanging sideways out of her mouth as she looks from him and back to me.

My face feels hot, probably because I'm embarrassed and defeated. I shouldn't have gotten my hopes up for the bunkhouse, and I definitely shouldn't have told Kase about it until I checked it out. He's going to be so disappointed. I can get over it, but explaining it to him will be a challenge.

"I have to go," I tell him. "I'm sorry about what happened at the tavern. It can't happen again."

He just smiles and shakes his head at me, those damn eyes on me the whole time. "Darlin', you and me both know you're not sorry about kissing me. In fact, I think we should do it again. And again."

I huff. "Whatever, Ty." I turn around and storm back to the ATV where Kase is sitting. Who does he even think he is calling me out like that? He doesn't know me.

"Mellie, wait..." Ty calls as he starts after me.

"Momma, we don't get our new bunkhouse?" Kase asks, disappointed.

"No, honey. We're going back to the garden shed. It'll be okay."

"But I wanted my own bed and room for my toys." He starts to cry, feeling as disappointed as I am.

"I know, honey." I start the ATV and shoot one last irritated look at Ty, standing with his massive arms crossed over his equally massive chest, before I drive away.

Back to square one. No bunkhouse. No Ty. But damn if he didn't look good. Even I want things I can't have with him, I shouldn't have kissed him at the tavern the other night.

I pull my cart behind me as I head to the next room to clean, my romance audiobook playing through my headphones, just about to get to a juicy scene.

Just then, Logan jogs over and waves. "Mellie, can I talk to you for a second?"

I press pause. "Sure, what's up?"

"I'm sorry about the bunkhouse. It was a misunderstanding. Evan didn't know that I'd rented it out to Ty. I didn't know you were interested," he says, looking like he feels bad.

"It's okay, I understand. I can still plant my gardens out

there in that area, though, right?"

If he says no, I don't know what I'll do. I've already mapped everything out for that area, so if he says no, it's all a wash. The land that the gardens are on is technically Logan and Allie's, but since the inn and that property are side by side, the family basically just shares it all.

"Of course. Allie's excited to help with the farmers' market, and she's hoping you'll let her set up a table to advertise the bakery."

I smile at Logan, grateful for him letting me use the land. Logan is so generous, and him and Allie make the best couple. They've been through a lot, though, and they've earned their happiness. They got married amid a custody battle against her ex who was trying to steal Caleb from her and take him back to California. Luckily, that didn't happen. Watching them go through all that weighed heavily on me, reinforcing that I will have to face my own situation sooner or later. Seeing Allie get through everything she did gave me hope for my own situation, though. Preston is right about making sure Kase and I are legally protected.

And honestly, the garden shed is more than fine. When the greenhouse is done and the plants are out, we'll hardly be there anyway. "Thanks." I sigh with relief. "That will be awesome for her. I appreciate it."

It's not far from the truth. I have no idea what I'm doing and need all the help I can get. I'm building a future for Kase and me. I'll just have to make the garden shed work for now. Ty can have the bunkhouse.

I guess one perk of him living out there is I might run into him from time to time. There's nothing wrong with being friendly with him from a distance.

The problem is that now that I've kissed him, I can't imagine not kissing him. What have I started?

CHAPTER 5

~

Mellie

I'm just wondering how such a tiny thing
like you can have such a big attitude.

People suck. And the people that you pay to come put together your secondhand greenhouse who end up taking your money and not showing up? They're the worst. Lesson learned. More plants, fewer people. I'll just figure it out by myself.

I huff as I look around at the dirty piles of greenhouse pieces. I drag sections at a time and attempt to put them together like a puzzle. I almost just ripped a hole in my jeans with one of the pieces, so things are going well.

I pause to wipe the sweat forming on my forehead. I consider stripping off my pants and shirt to do this quickly in my underwear. I'm wearing one of my nicer shirts and my only good pair of jeans, so I'd like to protect one of my only good outfits. I don't really have any extra money right now for new clothes and I can't risk it.

What the hell? It's Sunday afternoon and no one's around. If I can do this quickly, I can be out of here before long, I lie to myself, knowing damn well this is going to take me a very long time to finish on my own. Probably a week of every evening when I could be working on something else out here. This not going the way I planned put me way behind on my already tight schedule.

I kick my ratty sneakers off and yank my jeans down, then pull my shirt over my head. I fold them neatly over the seat of my ATV. I'm wearing faded gray cotton granny panties and a faded black racerback sports bra. Like a swimsuit, right?

I slide my feet back into my sneakers and tighten my ponytail. I already feel so much better. I can do this. I don't need them to put this together for me. Let's do this, I repeat, trying to motivate myself as I go back to putting together this impossible puzzle.

I think about my old life in the suburbs and my new rural life here at the inn. I look around at the rows and rows of gardens and think about how many people we can feed with the food I'm growing here. Vegetables I grew from seeds.

Satisfaction fills me at the sense of purpose I feel every time I come out here.

Every time I make something grow, it's like my own personal revenge. Like a giant fuck you to Bradley with every good thing that happens to us. So, I make it my mission to make sure good things are happening for us every single day. Because if there's one thing that I've learned in the past year, it's that I am the creator of my own story. I can do whatever I want, and this life is what I've made it. Bradley no longer gets to be a part of it.

After the episode in the front yard, Bradley didn't allow us to go out front anymore, and the only time we could even go outside was for a short while in the backyard every so often. Not enough time to get anything done, like planting a garden.

I used to believe that if I just tried harder, it would get better. Spoiler alert: it never did. It always got worse. Always one step away from wondering if it would be my last, I thought for a long time that maybe it really was my fault. If I'd kept the house cleaner, was more attentive to Bradley, was prettier, dressed nicer, it would get better. I got so tired of working so hard to be so damn perfect, and it never mattered. It was exhausting. Life shouldn't have to be that way.

One of the last straws was the distinct memory of Kase and I hiding under the stairs in the closet when Bradley was drunk, raging and destroying the house.

Oddly enough, there's a closet under the stairs inside the main inn that's similar to the one in our old house. When I first got to the inn, I used to tense up every time I'd walk by it. The memories would flood back to me, and I'd almost have a panic attack. Evan saw it happen one day, and he asked me what was wrong. When I explained, he immediately hired a contractor to come in and turn it into a small, hidden play area for the boys and kids that were guests at the inn, with toys, a small TV mounted on the wall, and a bookshelf. Hopefully Kase doesn't remember that closet in the old house and just has these new memories of a happy play space.

I think back to what Preston said about helping and I wonder if maybe I can finally put this all behind me for good. I'm just dreading it, scared of the unknown.

I pause to drink some water and tilt my head up to the sky as I chug. Sweat is pouring off me. I'm going to need a shower so badly, but I need to get this done while there's still daylight, and while Kase is otherwise occupied with Caleb. When I have uninterrupted time to work like this, I try to get as much done as quickly as I can.

Something licks the back of my leg, making me shriek and jump. "Oh my God, what...?"

I look down to see a familiar gray Pitbull sitting at my feet and looking up at me, wiggling her little tail, her tongue sticking out as usual. Nova. Which means if the dog is here...

Oh. My. God.

And there he is.

He stands frozen at the clearing by the greenhouse, his eyes huge and fixed on me.

And suddenly I'm irritated. Irritated by how handsome he is and how he stirs up things in me that I don't need stirred. *Liar*, my brain practically shouts at me.

"Oh, it's you, the bunkhouse thief." I place my hands on my hips and stare right back at him. Two can play this game.

He says nothing, just cocks his head like he's thinking. Why's he looking at me like that? He thinks he can just stand there and stare at me? No.

"Shouldn't you be enjoying your bunkhouse?" I glare. Even though I'm mad at him, he's still *very* good looking, and he makes me really nervous. So, he's hot and he can kiss. Big deal. He and his dumb dog stole our dream of living in the woods with the gardens all around us.

He just stands there, his ball cap pulled low. His shaggy hair in need of a trim, sticking out of his cap, wearing a white hoodie with a beer logo on the front and worn jeans and boots.

But I have already had my life destroyed by a man. No, thanks. Not going back for seconds. This one can go in the Not Going To Happen pile. Like the rest of my dreams that didn't work out. Bye, Ty.

"How tall are you?" he asks with a smile and a southern drawl.

"Five-three, why?" I grit my teeth, narrowing my eyes at him.

His hands shoved into his pockets, he rocks back on his heels with a smirk. "I'm just wondering how such a tiny thing like you can manage such a big attitude." He looks amused, not even looking bothered by my jabs. He's not relenting, he's just giving it right back to me. And it is *hot*.

"Oh, so you want to try to be funny?" I retort sharply, glaring at him.

"Is it working?" He crosses his arms over his chest.

"No," I snap, rolling my eyes as I stalk over and drag another heavy piece toward the pile that should resemble a greenhouse but currently looks like a makeshift fort an eight-year-old built out of popsicle sticks and rubber bands.

"What are you even doing?" His eyes scan the mess I'm making.

"Isn't it your bedtime? Or did you just wake up?" I ignore his question. I'm not even sure why I'm being so mean to him, but he's stirring up things in me that I don't know how to process right now, so this is what he gets.

"I did just wake up. I work nights," he muses with a grin.

A low growl rumbles through the dog and she rolls on her back and puts her paws in the air.

"What's wrong with your dog? Why's she acting like that?"

"Nova's just goofy. Something you can relate to." He reaches down to scratch her belly.

"I'm *not* goofy." Now I'm annoyed. Who does he think he is?

"Darlin', you're out here gardening in your underwear. You're all sorts of goofy."

I freeze, my face flushing and heart pounding. *Shit.* I want to dig a hole, crawl in it, and cover myself with dirt. I forgot I wasn't wearing clothes. And I've been giving him this huge attitude. In my underwear. In my freaking underwear! *Oh. My. God.* Kill me now.

I rush over and snatch my shirt and jeans off my ATV and quickly pull them on. I want to get far away from here right now.

"Don't stop on my account," he drawls. "I wasn't complaining." But he's turned around and giving me space to put my clothes back on like a perfect gentleman, which irritates me even more. Why does he have to be so damn perfect?

I point at him, which is pointless because he can't see me with his back still turned. "This is your fault. If I had that bunkhouse for me and my son, I could garden out here anytime I wanted and change my clothes quickly whenever I needed, and this wouldn't be happening. But, no, you and your stupid dog stole it from me!" I shout.

Nova lets out another whimper, rolls over, and covers her

snout with her paws.

"What do you have against my dog? Everyone likes my dog," he says casually, with a hint of laughter in his voice. Of course he's laughing at me. Of course.

"I highly doubt that." No chance I'm about to admit that I do really like Nova.

"Let me help you," he says finally as he turns and looks at the mess like he's mentally trying to put together a puzzle. A puzzle I've been working on for over an hour and have made no progress on.

"I don't need your help. With anything. Enjoy your bunkhouse and your life."

His face softens. "I'm sorry about that. I didn't know you wanted it, I swear."

I stare at him, my rage beginning to burn out. I want to be mad at him, but he's making it difficult with his soft tone, charming eyes, and good looks.

I don't deserve his kindness. I've been so mean to him. Of course, it's not his fault he got to it before me. Now I soften, releasing the breath I didn't even realize I'd been holding.

"And you can use the bunkhouse anytime you need to change or do anything back here," he says, making me feel even more like a jerk.

I sigh with defeat. "I'm sorry I've been so mean. But to be fair, I'm just really disappointed about the whole housing situation."

"Understandable. Let me make it up to you. Why don't you and Kase come over for dinner sometime?"

I look over at him. He asked for Kase to come, too, so it's not a date. Maybe what happened at the tavern was a lapse in judgement. I can't let anything sidetrack me right now.

He's looking at me now like he's taking me in and I don't like it. Okay, I do. No. Yes. Ugh. See? I can't even think around him.

"What?" I ask as I put my hands on my hips.

He cocks an eyebrow. "So why *are* you gardening in your underwear?"

"Ugh." I cover my face in embarrassment. "If you must know, I didn't want to get my one nice outfit dirty, and I didn't think anyone else would be out here."

He nods as if what I just said makes complete sense. "What do you have against me and Nova?"

"I don't have anything against you. You just confuse me."

And his dog makes me miss Sassy so much it hurts, but how can I explain that to him? It hurts too much to even remember, let alone talk about it out loud to someone who can't know our past.

One night, Bradley took off with Sassy in his truck and came back without her. I asked him where he took her, and he said that next time it would be me that he'd take somewhere and not bring home. He ended up bringing her back a week later, and I never found out where he'd taken her. All I know is that when she came back, she was scared. I still miss her, and it makes me sick to my stomach to think about what Bradley is capable of with her left there by herself. I wonder if he even still has her.

"Nova seems to really like you," he offers, I guess trying to lighten the mood.

I cast my eyes down, not sure what to say. I'm embarrassed, and I feel like I can't go back and make it right.

"I need to go. I'm sorry. I'll stay out of your way."

"What about dinner?" he calls.

"I can't. I'm too busy, I'm sorry."

I jump onto my ATV before he can say anything more to me.

We've got a lot at stake here with this life I've worked hard to build for us at the inn. This guy could be trouble, something I don't need any more of. I need to be more careful. I let my guard down, and I can't afford to do that again.

CHAPTER 6

~

Ty

Could I build something with her
around all these secrets?

As I watch Mellie drive off, Nova whimpers at my feet. "I know, baby. She's wild, isn't she?" I pick up a stick and throw it for her. She runs to retrieve it, then drops it back at my feet.

This girl is simple, wild, beautiful, and real, but she completely baffles me. I want to get to know her better, but she's making it feel next to impossible. I thought we had something going, but she seems to really dislike me now.

"Maybe you stand a chance, Nova. Maybe you're the way

to this wild lady's heart." She leans into my leg. I guess it doesn't really matter anyway. I can't commit to anyone here since I'll be leaving when the job is up.

"I don't know how anyone could not like you, Nova," I say to my dog as she tilts her head. "You are the best girl, you know that?"

She yips in response and then darts off to chase a rabbit.

I walk over to see what Mellie was putting together and realize it's supposed to be a greenhouse. The way she has it set up, I can tell right away that it's not safe and it's not going to hold up. I examine the haphazard structure more closely and realize she has some of the top pieces on the sides and the side pieces on the top. It's an easy fix, it'll just take a little time to get it set up correctly and safely.

I begin to sort the pieces and put them in piles, like giant glass Legos with sharp edges. I'm used to fixing things daily, but this was probably overwhelming for her. She's tiny, and some of these parts probably weigh as much as she does. Not that she's not tough—I'm sure she could handle it if she had more time and the right clothes on. Or any clothes on, for that matter.

It is hot out here putting this together, so I strip off my hoodie and t-shirt, but unlike Mellie, I keep my jeans on. I smirk. It was funny seeing her building this in her underwear. I thought she was beautiful before, but now that I've seen her practically in nothing? Smokin' hot. I have a suspicion that life with Mellie is never dull. She seems funny, and surprises me with something new about her every time I see her. But still, there's pain and fear sometimes behind her eyes, and that's what gets to me. Who put that there? That's what I intend to find out.

I finish sorting the piles and get to work on the building. It's just before dark when Nova lets me know it's well past her dinner time and she's ready to go home. The greenhouse is finally finished, but I'll come back and check it over in the morning when the light is better. At least now she won't get hurt when she comes back to it, and this will hopefully make her not as mad at me anymore.

I like her, what's confusing about that?

"Come on, girl. Let's go eat. I'm starving." Nova happily trots with me back to the bunkhouse. This is the worst part of my day: coming home to an empty house. I want a family to come home to. The smell of food cooking, the sound of kids playing, a wife excited to tell me about her day. I want a kiss hello, a bear hug goodbye. Snuggles at night when it's cold. A hand to hold onto. I'd give anything for all of that. For me, it's the little things. Always has been.

Instead, I pour a can of soup into a pot and heat it up on the stove, then pour myself a big glass of sweet tea. I feed Nova and freshen up her water, thinking about Mellie again. I'll leave her alone if that is what she really wants, but something tells me it's not.

I do feel bad about taking the bunkhouse. Honestly, it's too big for just me. It has three bedrooms and two bathrooms. I wonder if it could work for us to live here together. I work nights and she works days, so we'd probably not even see each other that much, although I wouldn't mind seeing them.

I sit down at the table to eat my soup while I scroll through my phone. The soup tastes disgusting, and I can't help but wonder who decided, hey, let's put tasteless slop in a can and sell it? Gross. I toss it and rinse out my bowl, deciding to grab something on the way to work.

I hit the shower, then put on my coveralls. When I sit to put on my boots, Nova jumps in my lap, realizing I'm leaving. I know she hates being alone here, and I hate it for her.

"I know, girl, just go to sleep when I'm gone. I'll be back in the morning." I kiss her on her snout and she whines, leaning into me.

My phone rings in my pocket as I head out to my truck. I don't recognize the number, but I answer it anyway.

I stop at a drive-thru for a burger and fries, then head to the parking lot of Larkin where I sit in my truck and eat my food before my shift.

As I walk in, I see stacks of pallets and wonder if I could snag some of those to build something in the greenhouse for Mellie to put her plants on. I shake my head. Not my problem. I shouldn't think about her anymore. But that's the problem... I can't help it. She's gotten under my skin and now I think about her all the time. Could I build something with her around all these secrets?

Because, clearly, we both have 'em.

CHAPTER 7

Mellie

Oh, this is going to be good...

"What do we even know about this guy? He's impossible," I say as I set down a plate of brownies with a little too much force, one of them bouncing off the plate and landing on the table. I'm still irritated about my run-in with Ty and I need to talk about it with my friends.

Beth and Allie stop talking and stare at me. "Well, hello to you, too. Who are we shit talking about?" Beth snatches up a brownie and takes a bite.

"Ty. Who else has rented the bunkhouse?" I huff, exasperated.

Allie chuckles and takes a sip of her wine. "You didn't seem too bothered about Ty when you were kissing him at the tavern the other night. You didn't even eat dinner you were too busy to come up for air."

I put my face in my hands, not realizing how much of that they were paying attention to. "Okay, so he might be easy on the eyes and a great kisser, but he's also impossible." My face flushes at the memories of him kissing me.

"*Might*?" Beth scoffs. "There's no 'might' about it. Ty's a bona fide smoke show. And he's good with his hands, if you know what I mean."

Allie wrinkles her brow at Beth. "How do *you* know he's good with his hands?"

"Duh," Beth says, shaking her head. "He's a mechanic. He knows what he's doing."

"What? Are you insane? This is so complicated, and not what I need." I gape at her.

"Oh, it is most definitely what you need," Allie says, a smug smile on her face. "A hot, blue-collar mechanic to check under your hood. Yes, you definitely need that."

Beth and Allie burst out laughing so hard, they look like they can't breathe. I'm so glad they're enjoying themselves, because this is stressing me out.

"Absolutely not. Especially after what happened." *And shit.* I've said too much.

"Wait, what happened? Did I miss something?" Allie

reaches over and swipes the brownie that fell off the plate and takes a bite. "These are good. Did you make these?"

I roll my eyes. "Like I bake. I swiped them from Sasha."

I learned a long time ago from my ex, naturally, that I'm a terrible cook. I made spaghetti and garlic bread one time. When Bradley came home, I remember him walking into the kitchen and saying it smelled good. I was excited that I finally got something right.

Then he took in the frozen garlic bread and store-bought spaghetti sauce and got so angry. "You can't make anything homemade, can you? You're so lazy. I work all day and come home to frozen food and sauce from a fucking jar."

I had said I was sorry and explained that I'd wanted to make a quick meal so we'd have more time to spend together afterward.

"Why would I want to spend time with someone who is so fucking lazy? What do you even do all day? Nothing. You do nothing. I bust my ass for this family, and you can't even make me a decent fucking meal when I come home."

Having Sasha cook and Allie bake here so that I can get by without screwing up any cooking and remembering those days has been a relief. Having delicious meals ready for us every day might not be much to some people, but it has been nourishment to my soul.

I shift back to the present. "It's just bad. I can never show my face around Ty ever again," I say, hoping that they won't ask further questions.

Beth and Allie both turn to look at me, and Beth pushes her glasses up on her nose, tilting her head expectantly.

Wrong. I should have known better.

Reluctant to tell them, I slink down in my chair. "Okay, something did happen." I lean forward and put my face in my hands. It's getting warmer as embarrassment grows.

"What?" they both say at the same time.

"He saw me in my underwear," I squeak.

"What? Where were you at in your underwear?" Beth wonders.

"If he's a creep, I'll—" Allie starts to say as she steps up from the table, ready to pounce.

I hold up my hand to interrupt. "He didn't do anything wrong."

"Oh, this is going to be good," Beth says, rubbing her hands together with glee.

"I was out trying to put the greenhouse together—"

"Which looks great, by the way," Allie interrupts. "I saw you got it all done. Great job."

"What? It's not done." I shake my head, confused. "I still have so much work to do on it. It's a mess."

"Well, it looks good to me. It looks like you can even start moving your plants in."

That greenhouse is most definitely not even close to being done. "What do you mean?"

"I can't imagine what else you would need to do to it, but anyway," she waves at me, "go on, tell us more…"

I shake my head again, not really getting what she's seen that I haven't, but I'll get back to that in a minute. "Anyway, I was wearing my best jeans and a nice shirt and didn't want to mess them up, but I didn't have time to go all the way back to the garden shed to change, so I stripped down to my underwear to keep my clothes nice."

Allie's eyes are wide. "Oh my God. That's hilarious." She begins to laugh so hard she hiccups, which makes Beth laugh even harder. *Ugh. These two.*

"I'm glad you think so," I deadpan.

"And then what happened?" Beth asks, making a goofy, dreamy face. "Did he bone you up against the greenhouse?"

"Yeah, girl, we're definitely living vicariously through you," Allie interjects. "I'm happily married, but have you seen that man?" She looks at Beth, and Beth smirks and nods back. "He's built like a unit."

"Continue…" Beth says, smiling expectantly.

"That's it. It was humiliating, okay? Now I can't show my face around him. My heart can't take the awkwardness." I realize I'm exaggerating a little here. It was embarrassing, but now that I'm saying it all out loud after it's over, I even want to laugh.

"What kind of underwear were you wearing?" Beth interrupts.

"Why does that matter?" I stammer.

"Was it your hot underwear or your granny panties? It most definitely matters." Allie nods in agreement.

"Granny panties," I mutter. "It's all I own."

"Ugh, well, we're fixing that," Allie declares.

Beth agrees. "Yeah, we are. Every girl must have emergency sexy panties for when you garden in your underwear."

"You two are absolutely no help," I say, exasperated, but deep down I'm so relieved to share this with them. It's been so nice having Allie and Beth as friends to laugh with and do life with during the hard times.

I've missed this. I had friends once—Piper and Nora. They were dental assistants at the clinic where I worked. We had lunch together every day, did secret Santa's at Christmas, and we took turns bringing in coffees for everyone. And then I had to quit, which meant quitting being friends with Piper and Nora, too. At first, they'd text and call, but it got harder and harder to make up new excuses on why I couldn't meet up with them. A few times, they mentioned they were worried and wanted to check on me. Bradley didn't want me to be friends with anyone, though, and then he eventually stopped letting me leave the house altogether.

I felt so lonely and isolated, which is when I started crafting to cope. I've learned to be creative with what I have around me, and I can stretch a dime into next week. That's how these gardens got built on a budget.

I'm still confused about the greenhouse, though. "Wait, are you sure it's done? There's no way."

She shrugs. "Roof and all. I was impressed. I figured the guys you hired showed up after all. Or you got Pete or one of the guys to do it."

"They most definitely did not show up, totally stiffed me. I'll check with Pete."

Allie shakes her head. "What a bunch of dicks."

"We can go see it if you want?" Beth offers.

"Okay," I agree, anxious to see it for myself.

Just then, I hear a vehicle pull up. Allie looks out the window and bites her lip. "Guess who?" She has a big smile on her face as she looks back over at me.

Oh God. Nope. I can't see him after the underwear incident. "No, no, no. You're kidding me." I stumble out of my chair and look out the window.

Beth looks over, too. "Yep, he's going to workout in the barn with the guys. Logan put together his own home gym out there, and Evan and him have been lifting together. They invited Ty today. Whoo, it's going to be smokin' hot out there."

"This is what I'm talking about. It's not good," I say, but secretly, I'm curious. Ty did look pretty good the other day when I saw him shirtless. I mean, what could another looksee hurt?

"Hopefully they take their shirts off this time," Beth says

with a sigh.

"Gross, that's my brother." Allie fake gags.

"Kill me now," I mumble, still thinking about the next time I'll have to interact with Ty. Maybe he forgot I was in my underwear. A distant memory he can't access. Yeah, I'll hope for that.

"Don't get your granny panties in a wad, Mel," Allie chirps.

Both dissolve into a fit of laughter again, and despite my embarrassment, I can't help but smile. They do make me laugh, and it's never boring with them, that's for sure.

"Hey," Allie pipes in. "Let's go check out your greenhouse while they work out." She slides into her boots by the door. "Boys!" she calls to Kase and Caleb. "Go out to the barn with the guys while we're going to the greenhouse."

We head out through the mudroom toward the barn. The doors of the barn are wide open, and sure enough, they're in there lifting away. They aren't shirtless, but Ty does look good. *Damn it.*

"Hey, guys." Beth waves as we walk by. All three turn and wave back and we head down the dirt path to the cabin and pole barn that is probably half a mile down the road.

I take this time to keep my head down and not make eye contact with any of them, hoping that I'm invisible and all they see is Allie and Beth. Not me. Nope, nothing to see here. Luckily, they don't make a move to make conversation and just continue working out. I'm relieved as we head down the road to the garden area.

"You all set for your grand opening?" I ask Allie as we walk.

"It's finally almost done. The kitchen is about ready and we're working on the dining area now. I can't wait for you guys to see it all finished."

"I can't wait. You've been working so hard. It's going to be amazing."

"Thank you for helping with the decorating, Mellie. I had no idea you were so talented with all of that. It turned out amazing, and the plants are really making the place pop."

"Of course," I murmur. "Happy to help."

"Let me know if you need any help sample testing," Beth offers up. "The baby and I don't mind being a part of the quality control team."

"I sure will. We have samples to test later at the house."

Just then, we round the corner, and there it is. The greenhouse. Fully finished. Gleaming in the sun. All the pieces put together correctly. What the hell? It even looks bigger than I'd thought it would be.

"Oh, wow." We open the door and stand inside.

"See? Finished," Allie says with a wave of her hand.

"Did Logan or Evan do it?" I ask.

"No one said anything to me." Beth shrugs.

"Maybe it was Pete," Allie suggests. "Either way, it looks great, and you can finally make more room in your garden shed to live."

"This is incredible," I whisper, looking around. "I'll figure it out and thank them."

"Maybe it was Ty." Beth wiggles her eyebrows up and down dramatically. "I can think of a few ways you can thank him."

I roll my eyes but shake my head with a smile.

"Maybe this is his way of thanking *you* for giving him a show in your granny panties," Allie teases.

"We don't know if Ty did this. And why would he?" I groan.

I look around and take it all in as the sun is getting ready to set. It's gorgeous out here. The gardens will be perfect.

CHAPTER 8

~

Ty

Time is running out for me
here in Freedom Valley.

"I'm glad you set this up," Evan says, scanning the workout equipment in Logan's barn.

"Thanks. This used to be the cow milk room," Logan replies as he finishes a set on one of the benches and switches places with Evan.

"What are you going to do with the rest of the space?" Evan asks, looking up at the high beams.

"Host your wedding this fall," Logan responds with a grin, wiping sweat off his forehead with a towel.

Evan laughs. "And then what?"

"I don't know, whatever your sister wants. The bakery's almost done. That's been taking up most of our time, but it's all coming together. Then I'm not sure what."

"Well, I like getting away from the inn for a while and getting a workout where not too many people are around," Evan says.

"You're welcome any time." He looks at me. "I'll give you the code to the door too, so you can use it whenever you want."

"Thanks, man, I'd take you up on that." I take a swig of water before heading to the pull-up bar.

"So, how's it going over at Sam's?" Evan asks.

Evan misses nothing, and I know I need to earn his approval still. What I've learned about Evan is that he's a former Marine and he is fiercely protective of his family, the inn and their staff, and this town. He's a pillar of the community, and to have his approval goes a long way around here. Plus, he seems like a good guy, one I'd like to be friends with.

I answer cautiously, "I like it."

"Where were you staying before the bunkhouse?" Evan adds weights onto one of the bars.

"I rented the apartment above Sam Sr.'s shop, but he needed it back for his son. That's when Logan offered up the bunkhouse."

Evan pauses his lifting. "Wait, so Sam Jr. is back?"

"Yeah, he's working mostly at night at the shop."

"Interesting," Evan mutters.

I wonder if they are old friends. I've only ran into Sam Jr. a few times, but he seems friendly yet quiet, and I get the impression he likes to keep to himself.

I glance over at Logan who is adding weight to his rack. It's been hard to make friends in town, being the new guy can get lonely and work keeps me busy, so I've decided that I want to get to know these guys better. It can't hurt to learn more about people in this town and make new friends while I'm at it. Plus, Mellie's usually around, so that's a perk.

"You're new here, too. How do you like it?" I ask Logan, relieved to switch the focus.

"It's been great. I don't really feel new, though. Beth and I work together and have been friends for a long time. Allie and I just got married a few months back, and I love being Caleb's stepdad. Everything's really come together for us."

I don't miss the way Evan smiles at this. He spots Logan as he lifts without saying anything. That approval is what I'm aiming for, because if I have it, I might have an easier time with Mellie. Those two are best friends it seems.

"You guys have a great family here. You're very lucky." I set my water down to do more pull ups.

"I'm surprised Allie and Beth haven't played matchmaker for you yet," Evan says. "When Allie, Beth, and Mellie get together, look out."

"Exactly," Logan says. "It might end up like *The Bachelor,* only Freedom Valley edition, and they'll probably hold a singles auction for you."

"I try to keep to myself. Been busy with work," I tell them. Although, I wouldn't mind if they smoothed things over with Mellie for me and made her stop hating me. I don't say any of that out loud to them, though.

Evan then surprises me by just coming out with it directly. "What's up with you and Mellie?" He must be able to read the surprise on my face because he then quickly adds, "You two seemed close at McGuiness the other night."

Well, way to cut right to it, I guess. What *is* up with me and Mellie? I'd like to have the answer to that question myself.

"I like her. Not sure she feels the same, though. She's not very happy with me right now."

"About the bunkhouse?" Evan asks. "I didn't realize you'd rented it when I told Mellie about it."

"It's okay. I talked to her, and she was cool about it." Logan grunts as he dips under the weight of the bar.

"She's doing alright in the garden shed," Evan says defensively.

Interesting. Evan is protective over Mellie, and it makes me feel like he knows more about Mellie and her past. She works for him and lives on the property, so it makes sense she's opened up to him. I decide to dig a little to see what he says, put him on the spot.

"Didn't she move here about the same time I did?" I ask. "She's fairly new here, too, I thought."

Evan freezes a few seconds before going back to lifting. "Yep," he says nonchalantly.

I don't miss the way he tenses up when I ask. Anyone with eyes can tell Mellie has a past, I just didn't realize how deep it must be until now.

"So what's her story?" I ask, trying to sound casual.

Evan quickly changes the subject. "Hey, hand me that towel?"

"Sure," I say, tossing it to him.

"Look," he says, turning to me. "Mellie's like a sister to us. I like you. You seem like a good guy and all." He takes a deep breath. "But... just don't go there unless you mean it, okay?"

We hear footsteps crunching gravel outside before I can respond.

"Hey, guys," Logan says as Caleb and Kase race in. "Where are your moms?"

"Off giggling somewhere about you guys," Caleb says as he climbs up on a mini trampoline set up in the corner.

"They went to look at the greenhouse and told us to come here," Kase finishes as both boys begin to jump.

So she knows the greenhouse is done... I hope it makes her happy. I choose not to say anything about it, just keep doing my workout and listening, grateful for the interruption from

Evan warning me about Mellie. The problem is I don't know what I want with Mellie. I like her, but I don't know how this could work between us when I'm not going to be here permanently.

"What are your moms giggling about?" Evan asks the kids.

"Mom says Ty is cute and Beth says he's dreamy and Mellie says he's humiliating," Caleb replies with the raw unfiltered honesty that four-year-olds have.

Logan chuckles. "Oh, really," he says, looking over at me. "Making moves on my wife?" he jokes.

I hold my hands up. "Absolutely not," I reply with a chuckle.

Evan cuts his gaze to me. "Why does Mellie think you're humiliating?" He doesn't break his stare, and it's intimidating as hell.

I clear my throat and say quietly, "We had a little... incident."

Logan moves in closer to me so the boys don't hear. "What kind of incident?"

I choose my words carefully before I speak. If she tells them later, I don't want them to think I'm a creep or something.

"I was out for a walk with Nova, and we came upon Mellie working on her greenhouse."

Evan's eyes narrow. "And then what?"

"Well, she was gardening in her underwear. I still don't

fully understand why, but she was bothered by me living in the bunkhouse and she let me know it."

Evan's face freezes for a few seconds before he bursts into laughter.

Logan joins in. "That's freaking hilarious."

Relieved that they're taking it lightly, I explain, "She was mad. The worst part was that she *forgot* she was in her underwear while she reamed me. Then once she realized it, she left as fast as she could."

"I wish I could give her shit about this," Evan chuckles.

"Remember that time Mellie teased you about the older lady at the inn who had a crush on you and called you her personal bellboy? Mellie had found an old bellboy uniform at a costume thrift shop and left it hanging in your office as a joke."

Evan rolls his eyes. "Yeah."

"She needs a gardening uniform." Logan laughs.

"That's not a bad idea," Evan says. "Payback."

Logan walks over to the little drink fridge and snags three sport drinks. He tosses one to Evan and then one to me. He grabs a couple of juice pouches, opens them, and sets them on the counter for the boys.

"Thanks." I take a sip, standing in front of the fan for a second. I wonder if she's still mad at me. Maybe her seeing the greenhouse will soften her up.

We workout for a while longer and I think about how life

could be if I lived here, if I wasn't here just for the job. I'd have friends, maybe even a family like they do.

"Are they back yet?" I look over at Logan's house. It's a white, two-story farmhouse with black trimmed windows and a wide wraparound porch.

"Yep, I think so," Logan says.

"I should go so she's not uncomfortable." I pick up my towel and throw it over my shoulder.

"She'll be alright. You live here too now, so it's best you both get the awkward out of the way," Logan says.

Evan agrees. "Let's head over. My sister usually has something freshly baked."

We all head over, the boys trailing behind us. Logan opens the side door, and we step in. "Ace!" he calls, his face beaming.

"Hi, babe." Allie comes in and she leans up to kiss him. "How was your workout?"

"Good."

"Hey, stinky," Allie says to her brother, punching him lightly in the arm.

"Hi, Ty, come in. You're included in this. I can't decide what's going to make the final cut for the bakery menu," Allie says warmly.

"Hello," I say, stepping in and holding the door for the boys to pass through.

"What did you bake me?" Evan asks, ignoring her jabs.

"A whole menu sampler. I need your opinions on my current lineup, gentlemen. Who volunteers to be my taste tester?"

"Don't have to ask me twice," Evan says, walking toward the kitchen.

I've heard a lot of buzz about Allie's new bakery coming to town and I've heard she makes the best baked goods in Freedom Valley. "I'm definitely happy to help out." I follow them into the kitchen that looks newly remodeled with bright white countertops, dark walnut cabinets, and an exposed brick backsplash.

All I can focus on is Mellie. She won't acknowledge me, but I don't even care. Her hair is pulled up in a ponytail, her face makeup-free, making her look younger than she is.

"Hey, Mel, Ty's here," Logan says, nodding to me and reaching over for a brownie and probably trying to address the elephant in the room: me.

Evan puts his arms around Beth from behind, cradling her baby bump. I feel a pang of jealousy, and I wonder if he realizes how lucky he is.

My eyes drift over to Mellie, catching her watching me, and her eyes cut away quickly as if she's embarrassed. Beth says something quietly to her, and Mellie rolls her eyes as Beth and Allie giggle.

"What?" Logan looks back and forth between them.

"Oh, nothing. Mellie just needs someone to work on her..."

engine," Beth says. Mellie glares at Beth.

Evan looks confused. "What engine?"

Allie cuts in quickly. "The ATV."

"I can take a look." I shrug. I'm thankful that they've included me in their friend group, and I am a mechanic after all, it's the least I can do to offer to help them. Something tells me that engine is a metaphor for something else, but I'll play along.

"You really don't have to do that. My... engine is just fine," Mellie says, unable to look at me.

Allie and Beth look like they're struggling to breathe trying to hold back laughter. It's not working.

"What is wrong with you two?" Logan asks again.

They snort laugh, tears welling up in their eyes. Mellie isn't laughing. She just looks up at the ceiling and shakes her head.

Evan says, "Okay—" but he's unable to finish what he wants to say as his phone rings in his pocket. He pulls it out to answer it.

"What's up, Sash?" he asks as he heads into the other room to take his call.

"Okay, okay, let's be serious. It's tasting time," Allie says. "Is there anything you absolutely don't like?"

"I like mostly everything," I tell her.

"I need your honest feedback. Do you promise to give *honest* feedback?" She emphasizes the word "honest" and tilts her head at me, her piercing green eyes boring into mine.

Okay, so both of the Harpers are intimidating. Those green eyes they have make you feel like they can see into your soul. But she doesn't have to know how I feel about that.

"Absolutely," I say confidently.

"Okay, first, we have lavender lemon scones with vanilla bean icing." She cuts the treat into pieces and offers one to me.

One bite into it and it tastes like soap.

"Well?" she asks, hands on her hips.

Not wanting to offend her, I grapple with the right words.

"Ummm, it's... not my favorite. I don't think I'm a lavender guy, but I really like the lemon and the frosting part."

"Okay, try this one. A blueberry lemon muffin top." She cuts me another piece.

Nervous it might taste like soap, too, I bite into that one and feel relief when it doesn't. "This one is really, really good," I say, reaching for one more small piece.

Her eyes shine. "Thank you, I think so, too. I know lavender isn't for everyone, but some really like it."

Beth and Logan each reach for a piece and try one, nodding to each other. Logan says, "This is great, Ace. Going to be a total hit."

Mellie takes a muffin top and cuts it in half for the boys at the table.

Just then, Evan returns and says, "We have to go. All hands on deck at the inn."

"What happened?" Beth pauses and stares at him.

Mellie looks worried as she holds her son's hand and stands still, a look of terror frozen on her face. My first instinct is to go to her and protect her. I don't like seeing her like that—or anyone, for that matter. Evan says something quietly to her then speaks louder for the rest of us. "It's the garden shed. A leak from the loft to the bottom floor. A pipe must have broken, and water was running for a while out there before anyone noticed."

She looks visibly upset. "Oh, no. Was it the sink? We've tightened it so many times. It must have—"

"It's okay, we'll fix it," Evan says calmly. "It's not your fault."

My heart feels like it's being squeezed in a vice seeing her this vulnerable. Without even thinking, I jump in and say, "I can help."

Evan regards me for a minute then nods. "Thanks."

We all head out. Mellie walks over to her ATV and straps Kase in behind her. She starts it up and takes off, not looking back. Yep, a metaphor.

I get in my truck and follow them the short distance before I park and walk over to the garden shed. From the outside, it looks like a metal outbuilding, but inside is where the inn has their washer and dryers, linen carts, and supplies.

And it's a wreck. Everything is drenched, and it's going to probably need to be completely gutted.

Evan looks stressed and runs a hand through his hair. Beth puts her arm around him and asks, "What the heck happened?"

"A pipe burst, and part of the flooring collapsed," he tells her. "They're going to need somewhere to stay until we can get it repaired. And it's going to be a while from the looks of it."

"Okay, I'm going to go check our bookings and see where we can put them," Beth says, heading to the main building.

Sasha stops her. "Pete already looked. We're booked out for a few weeks now. Solid."

Allie sighs. "Our back rooms are still gutted at the farmhouse, and we hadn't planned on touching them until after the bakery renovations."

Margie says, "I have friends staying in my spare rooms. It's going to be at least a week before I can take Mellie and Kase in."

"Preston's been squatting in our guest room," Evan says. "We're full. Shit." He paces and runs his hand through his hair.

Mellie pulls up in the ATV and parks, then gets Kase unbuckled. She looks worried as she walks up and surveys the damage.

Seeing her this way, especially with her son, guts me, and I have no idea where this primal urge to protect her is coming from, but it's there. I want them to be safe. Somehow, she's become important to me and before I even give a second thought to it, I turn to Evan and say quietly, "What if they stay at the bunkhouse with me? There are two other rooms on the other side I'm not even using. I work nights and she works days, so I doubt our paths would even cross too often."

Logan shakes his head. "We couldn't ask you to do that."

"You didn't. I offered, and I don't mind. It's a big place for just me and Nova. I'm gone a lot between the factory and Sam's."

Evan looks at me skeptically and then his eyes narrow. "Why would you offer this?"

Logan nudges him. "What Evan means to say is, thank you for offering, and let's see what Mellie says." He shoots Evan a look and Evan shrugs his shoulders.

Mellie has tears in her eyes. Beth puts her arm around her and steers her off to the side to talk to her with Evan. I see her watch his face, listening to him talk, and then shake her head slightly. She then listens again and nods in defeat. He looks at me and his expression pretty much tells me that if I so much as even think about messing with her, I'm a dead man.

Beth takes Kase's hand to bring him over to the inn. He looks back at his mom, worried, then runs back to her to give her a hug. She hugs him back and kisses his head, her hand rubbing his back. He turns to go with Beth, but it doesn't look like he wants to leave his mom's side. He's so little and worried about his mom, but who worries about them? Where's his dad?

There's been no mention of him, and I'm thinking that there must be more of a story here. I'm not liking the read I'm getting from this, like he's not safe. I hope that's not the case, but it's just a feeling I have. Why else would she be so hesitant to start something with me? Who would leave these two? There's more that I am missing, I'm sure, but I still have no regrets about offering up the bunkhouse. They are good people, and I want to help them. That's it, right? *Shit. No, that's not it.*

I like her. And that's the damn truth.

When Kase and Beth leave, Evan walks back over to me. "They're going to stay with you, and we appreciate you offering." He stands there for a minute with his hands on his hips, not saying anything, and I know what he's thinking and probably trying very hard not to say. I already understand that Mellie is like a sister to Evan, and I'd probably react exactly the same way if I were in his shoes.

Not to mention there's a kid to think about, too. And judging from the concerns that seem to surround Mellie's past, they probably have reasons for being hesitant around a stranger.

"They'll be okay with me, I promise. I keep to myself, and I'll stay out of their way."

Evan looks like he's still trying to analyze me. *Okay, I get it, man.* I just look at him, nod, and head over to Logan who is motioning for me. If Evan really knew me and knew who I was, he wouldn't worry about me at all.

"Hey, can you back your truck in and we'll get as many of the plants out as we can? She's really upset about them. They lost pretty much everything they own tonight, which wasn't much to start with. I'm not even sure what is salvageable. This sucks, man."

I didn't even think about that. Everything they own, gone.

"Yeah, sure, no problem."

"Thanks. Allie and I are going to salvage what we can and then drop everything off at the bunkhouse."

I back up to the garden shed door. Tears streak Mellie's face as she pulls her plants out and loads them into the back of my truck. I want to give her a hug and promise her everything will be okay, but I stop myself. Instead,I start picking up bundles of plants beside her and packing them in. We don't say anything, just work side by side until all the plants and grow lights have filled up my truck bed.

"I think that's everything that can fit in this run," she says quietly, still not looking at me.

"Hey," I say, hooking a finger under her chin gently. She finally looks up and her green eyes are still full of tears. I want her to see that I'm here and I'm not leaving, that I want to help her. Give her some sort of peace and safety. I pull her into a hug and tuck her under my chin, hugging her tight and gently patting her back. I soften when I feel her arms come around me and hug me back.

"It's going to be okay. We'll get it all figured out, okay?" I reassure her.

She nods and then pulls away, heading over to get into Evan's truck to follow me. I drive out to the greenhouse and back the truck in.

It's messy in here, but it'll do until it's warm enough to put the plants outside in the garden. There are stacks of dusty tables folded in the corner from the pole barn, and I set up as many as I can before she comes in carrying a bundle of plants.

"I didn't know how you wanted them, but I figured we could just get them in here and figure it out when there's more light out."

She nods and says nervously, "Thanks for doing this. I know we're probably in your way, and I promise we won't be—"

I hold up my hand, and for a moment she flinches, then steadies herself. I step back and say, "I'm sorry. I promise you're not in the way. I'm sure Nova will love having you here, too. She gets upset when I leave her alone at night, so you'll be helping me out by keeping her company."

I'm not sure why she flinched, but I get the sense she might have been physically abused. I'm anxious to someday hear her story, but tonight, I just want her and her son to feel safe.

"I can help you with Nova." She hesitates for a minute and then adds, "Ty, can I ask you a question?"

"Yeah." I tuck my hands behind me and lean against the greenhouse wall, hoping she will be a little more disarmed and not as jumpy with me.

"Did you put this greenhouse together?"

I wasn't expecting that question and I'm not sure what to say, so I just shrug and nod.

"Why would you do that for me?" she asks, confused.

"I just wanted to help. You seemed overwhelmed with it, and I thought it might make you forgive me for taking the bunkhouse."

Her face softens and she says, "Thank you." She walks toward me, her eyes locked on mine, and she finally stops in front of me. She pulls my face down, steps up, and kisses me softly. I reach around and pull her closer, kissing her until she pulls back.

"What was that for?" I search her eyes.

"For putting my greenhouse together. No one has ever done anything like that for me before." Her face in the moonlight is as stunning and gorgeous as ever.

"Well, if that's all I have to do, do you have any more projects I can help with?" I joke as I cup her face and trace her freckles with my thumbs.

She laughs a little and turns to head back out. "No, but I'll let you know."

When we get to the truck, I open the door for her, and she pauses before she climbs in. "I'm sorry I was so mean."

"It's okay." I grin at her. "I still like you anyway."

She laughs again, the sweetest laugh I've ever heard. It's my new mission in life to make her laugh as much as possible every time I see her.

"I don't know why, but you seem like a good guy, Ty. Please be a good guy," she pleads. And there it is. Confirmation that her ex was not a good guy. Motherfucker.

I'll get to that topic later. But for now, I reassure her and give her what she needs in this moment. "I try every day to be a good guy. You've got nothing to worry about with me."

"Okay," she says, her eyes still locked on mine as if she's trying to decide whether she believes me or not.

I give her the code to the bunkhouse as we walk over, and she pulls out her phone and starts typing. "Saving that for later for when my brain doesn't feel like oatmeal," she explains. "I know I'll forget it."

"It's okay, you can text me if you forget or need something. Here, give me your phone. I'll put my number in."

She hands me her phone and I text myself. "There. Now we have each other's numbers."

I push open the door and step in, motioning for her to follow behind me.

"Wow, it's bigger in here than I thought," she says as her

eyes scan the kitchen and living area.

"It really is. This is why I think it will work out fine. The master bedroom is back that way," I tell her as I point to one end of the house. "Then there are two bedrooms and another bathroom that way, so there really is plenty of space for you both to stay here as long as you want."

"You said you work nights. I don't want to wake you up when you're sleeping."

"I sleep soundly, so I probably won't hear you unless you need help or something."

This is pretty much a lie. I hear everything, listen for everything. My real job is to be alert, see things and help people, but she can't know that. Yet. I want her to be relaxed and comfortable here. That's all that matters right now.

"We'll be fine. We go over to the main inn around eight in the morning and don't come back until after dinner, which is six or so."

"I'll be at work by then, so we will basically be like two ships passing in the night."

Sadly, I probably won't see her too much. I'll have to work around that.

"Where is Nova?" she asks, looking around.

"She's with Sam Sr. He's dropping her off here soon. He was watching her for me." I didn't want to tell her that he was trying to coax Sam Jr. out of the loft with Nova because he knows he's a big dog lover and thought she'd help cheer him up. Hopefully it worked.

"Kase is going to be so excited to spend more time with her."

"Well, I appreciate you looking after her when I'm working," I say, scratching my beard.

"What do I need to do with her when you're gone?"

"She just gets lonely at night. She whines and hates when I leave her alone, so just keeping her company is already a big help. Just give her snuggles, let her out to do her business, and make sure she's got food and water."

"Okay, I can do that." She seems to perk up with the thought of helping. She stares at me like she's still trying to figure out if I have an ulterior motive or something.

"What?" I ask quietly, stuffing my hands in my pockets and rocking back.

"I feel like I brought my complicated life over here and into yours." Her expression is filled with worry and hesitation.

"I think you're a lot less complicated than you think. Just try to be happy, yeah?"

She tilts her head, and I can tell she's thinking about something. "I don't know if it's that easy, but I think I can try."

"While you're here, I'll look out for you and your son. I'll keep you safe. Okay?"

I don't want to lie to her. She still doesn't know everything about me or even why I'm here in Freedom Valley. I can't tell her everything, and I can't make promises I can't keep.

"We don't need anyone to keep us safe. I can keep us safe," she says defiantly.

I'm gutted. I know I can't be honest with her yet, but I'm really hoping that when I finally am, she won't hate me. "Okay."

"Why do you like me and want to help me? You don't even know me." She stares at me, her freckles smattered across her cheeks, distracting me.

"Well, I *want* to know you, Mellie. I think you're beautiful, and you're a great mom. I like Kase, too. After the other night at the tavern, I think you like me, too, but if you're not ready yet, that's fine. I'll wait."

"You might be waiting for a while," she says. "I'm busy, and like I said... complicated. No man in his right mind would want to take this on," she says, waving at herself and her pile of bags.

"I've got time." I smile at her. And with that, I push off the counter and head out to my truck.

Shit. I want to help her, but I still have a job to do. The ball's in her court now, though. That doesn't mean I'm going to stop showing her I care and enjoy being with them for the time being, but I will try to wait for her to be ready.

I did lie, though. I don't have that much time. Time is running out for me here in Freedom Valley.

The truth is that whatever time I do have left, I'm going to give it to her.

CHAPTER 9

~

Mellie

This is just temporary, okay?

I don't even know what to make of all of this. Everything happened so fast, with the garden shed being damaged and ending up at the bunkhouse after all. Not the way I would have thought it would go, but here we are.

Ty does seem like a good guy, and I really want him to be, but I can't help feeling like I've been down this road before. Bradley pretended to be the most upstanding citizen. People used to come up to me and rave about what a great cop he was. They had no clue about the actual living hell Kase and I were going through at home. It was always a façade. One big, scary, *fake* life that we literally had to run from.

For some strange reason, I trust Ty when he says he's a good guy, and that scares me, because I never thought I'd trust another man. How could I? Yet Ty gives off completely different vibes than my ex-monster. We were young when we first met, and Bradley did a great job to overwhelm me with attention and flood me with fake affection in the beginning. And Ty? He's quiet, keeps his distance, and is nice to us. He doesn't push and doesn't seem to want anything from us other than to keep his dog company.

However, God help Ty if he ever tried to do anything to harm us in any way. There's one thing I do know living here this past year, and that's that the Golden Gable Inn is a safe space, and that everyone here would do everything in their power to protect us. I can't risk losing the safety that we have here. Without this place and these people, we have absolutely no one and nowhere to go. I'll do anything not to let Evan down after everything he's done for us.

I look around the bunkhouse and notice that Ty keeps his space tidy. A leash hanging on the hook by the door. Nova's dog bowls on the floor neatly filled and ready for her to come home and eat.

Just as I pull up to the shed to see what else needs to be done, Evan comes out and pats my shoulder. "Hey. We got out what we could. I'm sorry, Mel. We'll do what we can to get it fixed up so you can get back in. This is just temporary, okay?"

"Thank you. I will help clean it up, too." I'm already stretched thin with my time, but I want to help.

Evan shakes his head. "No. We've got this. We'll have a crew come out and get the laundry room functional tomorrow and gut whatever we need to and begin repairs. Just take care of you and Kase. Plus, now you can work on your greenhouse and gardens being closer out there. I guess you're in your bunkhouse after all." He grins and shrugs his shoulders.

"I guess." He seems cool about all of this, but I can't help but be worried this is somehow my fault. My mind races and my chest feels like it's full of lead. My memories immediately default to me being accused of being careless and the time in my life when everything was my fault with Bradley. I think about how we can fix this and how I can do better next time. I cautiously ask him, "Do you think I did anything to cause this?"

Evan seems calm and not worried about it. "No. It really was just a leak," he assures me. "The building's old, and it needs updating anyway. We'll get it even better than it was before. We have insurance. It's fine, I promise."

"Okay, I'm sorry." Relief fills me and I let out a deep breath.

"You get settled in over there?"

"Yeah. I even got all the plants set up. Did you know Ty put together my greenhouse?"

His expression softens. "No, but that was nice of him."

"He does seem nice."

"If at any time you need me, you just text me and I'll be there, and same for Logan," he says, giving me the impression that he doesn't fully trust Ty yet.

"Thank you."

"Alright, let's get this last load in the truck. Kase is down for the night so you can get things situated at the bunkhouse."

"Oh, that's great, thanks."

"I'll follow in the truck."

"Okay." I drive over to the cabin and pull in. A dark blue truck that I don't recognize is parked next to Ty's white one. Instantly, I tense up and get nervous. *Who else is here?*

Evan backs in and comes around to help me unload the bags into the house. I'm relieved when the door opens and Ty and Sam Sr. come out with Nova, who is excited to see me and Evan.

"Hey, Sam. This is the last of her stuff that we could get out. Want to lend a hand?" Evan glances over his shoulder before we both reach down to pet Nova, who is wagging her tail and leaning into me as I scratch her ears.

"Hey, sweet girl," I whisper, remembering the comfort that having a dog nearby can provide.

"Yeah, we've got this," Ty calls as he stands beside me. He looks at me, and like he's reading my thoughts, he says finally, "Mellie, have you met Sam Sr. yet?"

Okay, that was crazy. I feel like he just understood me, and I didn't even tell him I was apprehensive about someone I didn't know being here. How Ty and I can be in tune like we are, I don't understand. Somehow, he just gets me, and I like how it puts me at ease.

Trying to get back to a calm place, I say, "No, but I've seen you around town. It's nice to finally meet you, Sam," I say as he carries a few of my bags into the house.

Sam is the silver fox that everyone in town talks about. He has a son that he had pretty young, who I've never met before but have heard is back in town. I would put Sam in his mid-forties, but he doesn't look it, aside from his silver-gray hair. I've seen him play at the tavern with Evan a bunch of times. The ladies in town all like to jump at the chance to bring their vehicles in for him to fix at his shop, just so they can tell the story to their friends. I've heard Sam Jr. looks a lot like him, only he's in his twenties.

"You, as well. I'm sorry you're in a jam like this, but you're in good hands here with Ty."

For sure, I think to myself. Ty is definitely good with those hands—holding me on the dance floor, pulling me in for kisses that make me wonder what else they can do. *Oh, Mellie, rein it back in.* If I'm going to make it work living with him, I can't be thinking about him like this all the time.

Evan says to Sam, "I heard Sam Jr. is back. I need to reach out. How's he been?"

Sam Sr. looks a little defeated when he replies, "He came back a few weeks ago after getting out for good. He wants to lay low for a while. Needs some time. You know how it is."

Evan nods. "I get it. It's hard adjusting to civilian life again. I'll give him some time and then reach out soon."

"I think he'd like to see you. I don't know what to say to help him... Maybe you could get through to him."

Evan claps him on the back as they head back outside.

Once we get everything unloaded, Evan gestures at my phone and says, "I'll check in with you tomorrow."

I nod back. "Thanks."

"And later when we aren't so exhausted and can laugh about this, I'll get you a gardening costume." He grins and quickly pulls the door shut behind him before I can say anything back.

I turn to see Ty hiding a laugh before he straightens and looks away. "Of course you told him." I shake my head.

My face warms with embarrassment, but that's part of why I get along so well with Evan. Instead of treating me like a fragile doll, he teases me and considers me to be a normal person.

I'm not fragile. I'm rebuilding my life one brick at a time, and with every day that passes, I'm stronger than I was before.

I head inside to find Nova on my bed. "Oh my... What are you doing in here?" She responds by planting kisses on my face and jumps down, her little nub of a tail wagging so fast that her whole body wiggles.

Just then, Ty comes down the hall and stands in the doorway. "Come on, Nova." The dog scurries out after him. He runs a hand over his chin. "You need anything else tonight?"

I realize I'm frozen against the wall and slowly slide away. He gives me room and steps back. I'm relieved he doesn't push me and just meets me where I'm at. But damn if he's not scorching while he does it. And honestly, I don't mind him in my space, I'm just nervous. His smile with his perfect beard is just... Damn.

"Don't be nervous," he says softly. "I'm glad you're here."

"I'm just... I was wondering if you had an extra lamp." I look away, embarrassed. "I don't like the dark."

"Of course," he says softly and heads toward the other side of the house. I hear his footsteps coming back a few minutes later.

I'm scratching Nova's ears as she leans in and lays her head on me.

"She likes you," he says as he sets up the lamp.

"I like her, too."

"How about me?" he says, his tone flirty.

"Maybe someone else, too," I say back, putting my hands on my hips.

We both look down again and she's now lying with her

head on her paws, gazing at me in adoration. My heart softens, and I realize I'll probably fall for both this man and his dog.

"So, you're off tonight?" I ask, trying to change the subject.

"Yeah. I'm here if you need anything," he says kindly, but in a more serious tone. You bet I can think of a lot of things I might need from this man. I'm already treading on dangerous territory here.

"Thanks again, Ty." I walk over and kiss his cheek, standing inside the doorway so he knows it's a goodnight kiss. If I'm not careful, I'll pull him in and neither of us will be sleeping tonight. He pulls me toward him and kisses me softly, and then steps back.

"I'll see you tomorrow," he says, then snaps his fingers lightly and walks down the hall. Nova trots behind him, stopping every few feet to look back at me longingly.

I head into the other room through the jack and jill bathroom and see that it has a bed already made up and ready. Kase is going to love having his own room.

I know I'll sleep better knowing that everything is locked up, even if Ty's here, so I go out to make sure to lock the doors and windows out of habit. Then, I turn on every light in my room and bathroom because I can't sleep without the lights on.

It's not his job to keep me safe. It's mine.

CHAPTER 10

Mellie

What if I could let him in, too?

When my alarm goes off the next morning, I momentarily forget where I am. Still tired, I run my hand over my face and sit up. I change my clothes, deciding the quicker I clean rooms, the quicker I can get to my gardening.

I head out to the kitchen and hear scurrying paws as Nova comes to me and licks my hand, seemingly excited that I'm still here. She sits and stares up adoringly at me, and it reminds me of Sassy. I got through some of the hardest times because she was with me. She would snuggle into my side like she was hugging me, as if she knew I needed that.

And I did.

"You're so sweet. Like a little baby." I kiss Nova's head. She rewards me with a big sloppy kiss across my cheek.

Her eyes close and she continues to lean in as I scratch her ears. "Be good to my boy, okay? We could use a new friend."

"She could use some new friends, too," Ty says from the doorway. He's wearing jeans and a long-sleeved, white Henley that stretches over his massive mechanic forearms and broad chest. His cap is backward like it usually is. If I were in the market for a man, he'd be the perfect specimen. But I'm not actually looking for a real relationship, we just kiss sometimes, I lie to myself.

"Eavesdropping?" I tease.

"Observing. Coffee?"

"Definitely," I say with a grateful smile.

He takes down a light brown and navy, pottery-style mug off a hook and pours me a cup. "How do you take it?"

"With cream, please, if you've got any."

He walks over to the fridge and opens it. I notice it's bare inside except for the creamer and a few energy drinks.

"I'd say help yourself to anything, but there's not much. But whatever you find, you can have."

"Where's *your* coffee?"

"I don't drink coffee."

"What do you drink?" I ask in confused horror. People really exist without coffee?

"Energy drinks and water."

"Oh. So you made this coffee for me?"

"Maybe," he says with a grin as he hands me my mug. "I'm going to do some errands before I head to bed. I'll be working tonight so I probably won't see you, but you can text me if you need anything."

"Thanks," I say softly into my cup as I take a sip. It's good coffee, too.

He walks over and kisses me on the forehead, then gives me a quick wink before walking over and petting Nova. "Be good," he tells her as he closes the door behind him.

I look back down at her. "You look like you're always good."

Through the kitchen window, I watch Ty walk to his truck. *He made me coffee?* What's wrong with this man? What's wrong with me? I keep waiting for the other shoe to drop, but what if he's just a nice guy?

My phone buzzes, interrupting my thoughts. A text from my group thread with Beth and Allie.

Beth: How was last night? Did you settle in okay?

Allie: Yeah, we need details.

Beth: Did you see him shirtless? (Heart eye emoji)

Allie: Beth! You're practically married to my brother!

Beth: This is "book research" for my next romance novel.

Allie: (Eyeroll emoji)

I sigh and text back.

> **Mellie:** You both are ridiculous. (Smiley face emoji) I didn't see him shirtless. But he did make me coffee. And the dog might be my favorite.

Nova sits at my feet, her long tongue hanging out to the side in her usual goofy-looking grin. I instinctively reach over and stroke her velvety head.

My phone dings again with another text.

> **Allie:** When are you getting here? Sasha wants to hear deets too and she's making us omelets. We also got you something.

My stomach rumbles at the idea of breakfast. I finish my coffee and rinse the cup before placing it in the dishwasher. Ty's kitchen is very clean, and I want to make sure he doesn't feel like we're making a mess being here.

> **Mellie:** I'm on my way.

A few minutes later, when I pull up to the inn, Kase comes running out and hugs my leg. "Momma. How's the new bunkhouse?"

"It's good, baby. I can't wait for you to see it. It's just temporary while Evan fixes up our shed, but I think you're going to like it." I stroke his blond hair and rub his back. I learned my lesson getting his hopes up before, and I don't want him to get too comfortable since we won't be there long. "Did you sleep well?"

"Yeah. And Sasha made me Mickey-shaped pancakes, too," he says proudly.

"Oh, that's nice. I bet they were so yummy."

"Is Nova there?"

His excitement about the dog makes me happy. "She is, and I think she's pretty excited to see you, too."

"I can't wait! I can help with her, you know. I've been helping with Chip and Bossy!"

I wonder if he's forgotten Sassy. "That would be nice, honey."

"Allie says you have to spill the tea, whatever that means, so Caleb and I ate already so we can go paint with Grandma Margie."

My heart softens hearing him call her that. Margie treats Kase like her own grandchild and loves doing fun things with him. I'm so grateful for her. She's the only grandparent my son will probably ever have. Tears prick my eyes at the thought, in a mix of gratitude and relief.

"That sounds fun. What are you going to paint?"

"Dinosaurs," he says.

"Can you change first? I don't want you to get paint on your good shirt."

"You, too, Mom. Don't get tea on your shirt." The poor kid looks genuinely confused and I don't have the heart to explain to him that "spilling the tea" means telling the details.

Margie comes out and gives me a hug. "Sorry about your place, honey."

"I'm just sorry it happened." I hug her back. "Thanks for painting with him today."

"It's my pleasure. We've got dinos to paint, don't we, boys?"

"Yeah," the boys call back to her.

"Have a good day, honey. Get a good breakfast in you." It feels nice to have Margie care about me like she cares about Kase, like we are loved.

They go over to the path that leads to Margie's cottage as I enter the kitchen, my stomach immediately grumbling. The counters are covered in sausage, bacon, and cheese, and something sweet is baking. Guests take plates of food to the dining room and friendly chatter fills the air.

"Hey, Sasha," I call out. "It smells amazing in here."

The first day we walked into the inn and met Sasha, she greeted us with hugs and love. No questions asked. Just fed us, laughed with us, and make us feel like part of the family here. I've sat at this very kitchen counter and cried and laughed with everyone so many times I can't keep count. She's told us about her and Pete and their history of working at the inn. She gently prodded into my past but quickly realized she's better off focusing on our present when I wouldn't talk about it. She's become a protective mama bear to us, and I'd do anything for Sasha.

"Good morning, Mellie. Omelets, grilled blueberry muffins, and fresh fruit," Sasha says.

"Sounds good to me."

"I'll bring you a plate. You get settled, okay?" she asks as she walks by and pats my shoulder.

Sasha and Pete have been at the inn since Evan and Allie were young. I love when Sasha tells us funny stories from when they were little, and I like to tease Evan about some of his escapades. Like when he thought a skunk was a barn cat and he petted it in the dark and almost got sprayed.

Which reminds me I still need to get him back for the gardening uniform comment. I can't believe Ty told him about seeing me in my underwear.

I sigh and sit back.

"Why the long sigh?" Sasha asks as she flips my omelet in her cast-iron pan.

"Just been a long week."

"It's Tuesday." She laughs.

"You know what I mean." I grin. "Where's Allie and Beth?"

"They'll be back in a minute. They ran out to pick up some things from town."

Sasha pours me a cup of juice and sets it in front of me. "You need to eat more, honey. You work too much, and you don't take enough breaks. Gonna work yourself into the ground."

"I know. I just want to get everything planted so we can get the farmers' market up and running. Then I'll have more time."

"That's a lie and you know it." She laughs. "You'll always find stuff to do in those gardens. What do you have left?"

"I'm not sure. I need to make a new plan. Check everything over for damages. Get everything straightened out."

"The greenhouse looks great," Pete calls from the doorway, having just arrived from somewhere. "What else do you need help with? I know you won't ask, but I'm offering, you stubborn girl." He grins at me and slides his work gloves in his back pocket before planting a kiss on Sasha's cheek. "You know I would have helped you if you would have asked," he tries to scold me playfully, even though we both know he's a big teddy bear.

"I know. I just don't want to bother you with things I can try to figure out on my own. I know you're busy, too."

"I'm never too busy for you, kiddo. You need something, you just ask, okay?"

"Okay, thanks." I take a bite of my omelet, cheesy, warm, and comforting, and close my eyes. "Sasha, what do you put into these omelets? For the love of God, they're so good."

"It's one of the new seasoning blends I'm playing around with. I'm hoping I can sell some of my seasonings at your farmers' market, if you think that would be okay?"

"Of course. Everyone will love them. Especially the maple

bourbon. That's one of my favorites."

Pete wraps his arms around Sasha and gives her another kiss. "See you later, babe."

"Bye, love you," she tells him.

"Love you more," he calls back as he shuts the door behind him.

What Pete and Sasha have is total relationship goals. A solid, happy couple who love their life and love each other, happy and secure in their marriage. I dream of having even a fraction of that someday, but how can I ever risk that again?

"Penny for your thoughts," Sasha says. As close as we are to her, she and Pete don't know the details of our past, nor will they.

"Just that you and Pete are couple goals."

She laughs. "We're not perfect. Took us twenty years to get to this point, and we both sure had our moments along the way." She looks at me and says, "You'll find yours."

"I think I'm content with the way things are. I have to focus on Kase." I take the last bite of my omelet, and then resist my desire to lick the plate.

Sasha is a strong woman who doesn't do mushy feelings. It's one of the things that I love about her. She is who she is, and that's that. She runs this kitchen and takes no nonsense from anyone. She's not afraid to voice her opinions, but it's meant with love. She's the backbone of this inn.

The door opens and Allie and Beth come in. "Oh, good,

you're here." Allie smiles as she heads in my direction and sets down a few bags.

By the look on their faces, they're up to something.

"What's all this?" I ask before drinking the last of my juice.

"Your new clothes," Beth says. "And don't give me any grief. I wanted to, and you can just say, 'Thanks for the new sexy underwear for Ty.'" She says the last part in a high-pitched voice.

"I don't sound like that," I deadpan.

"Oh, okay, how about this." Allie affects a deep, husky voice, then adds, "Thanks, Allie and Beth! Now I can get laid by that sexy, blue-collar mechanic and—"

I hold up my hands and look around to make sure no one is around. "Okay, okay, stop. I don't sound like that either." I shake my head and laugh. God, I love them. It feels good to be comfortable being razzed by my friends. To have friends here is a complete privilege. After a year of being here in Freedom Valley, I feel pretty good about where we're at, knowing we're safe, no longer feeling like we're living day by day. The longer we're here, the better I feel about Bradley not finding me.

I feel guilty keeping my past a secret from Allie and Beth. I've let them in a bit, but I'm starting to wonder if I could open up even more now that I've been here awhile and feel confident that we're safe. I don't worry about them compromising our location, I just worry they'll look at me differently. I left the past behind and I kind of like that this is how they know me, as the new Mellie. They don't look at me with pity, and I can't help but ask myself if they would still look at me the same if they really knew the truth.

Beth is giddy as she starts pulling underwear out of her bag. "Here's what you need to be gardening in."

"What the heck are you talking about?" Sasha asks, then puts her hand up. "Wait, maybe I don't want to know." She hangs up her dish towel and walks over to the pantry, shaking her head.

Allie pulls out new jeans and two cute sets of overalls—one in a pretty shade of jade green and one in maroon.

"Oh, I love these," I whisper, holding them up. I've grabbed a few t-shirts and a pair of jeans for myself at the local thrift store in Freedom Valley, but I haven't gotten new clothes in so long. Especially ones like these, trendy and beautiful. It's such a luxury.

"You shouldn't have done this," I tell them. My heart feels so full as warm fuzzies buzz through me.

"We wanted to do something nice for you. You do so much for me by helping with Caleb, and you're like a sister to me, Mellie."

"We love you," Beth says. "I don't know what I would have done without you since I've been here. You've been there for me when I was at my worst, and when I came back you gave me a friendship that I'm so grateful for."

"I don't know what to say." I feel so loved right now. Overwhelmed, but loved.

"Let me love you," Beth says in a deep voice.

I laugh. "You're *so* weird."

"And that's why you love us." Allie grins. "Okay, I've got to get to the bakery before the contractors this morning. You good to keep Caleb today, Mellie?"

"Margie has them for now, and then I'll get them after work. I'm going to take them out to the gardens to play later." I clear my glass and plate from the table. "Thanks, ladies. I love you, guys."

"You bet, love you back," Beth says as she hands the bags to me.

"We love you more," Allie says as she blows me a kiss and I duck out back with all my new clothes, excited to try them on.

I get all my rooms clean and barely have enough time to swipe a bottle of water on my way out to the gardens when Sasha stops me. "Uh-uh. Freeze. Get back here, I have something for you."

I step back into the kitchen. Sasha hands me a sandwich wrapped in a napkin. "You can eat this on your way." Then she tosses me a bag of chips and a few baggies of carrots and cucumbers.

"Thank you," I call out as I wave and head out to the back of the property, thankful she thought to make me a to-go lunch.

I park in front of the greenhouse and reach into my bag to pull out the map I drew of my garden. I've redrawn these plans dozens of times and color-coded them with markers. It's been so fun to dream up what's growing where, what color of flowers, what vegetables, what fruits, and adjust when I find another little piece of land to add to it.

I finish up my lunch and take a sip of water. I wave curiously at Evan as he pulls up next to me and parks.

"Hi, what are you doing here? I thought your mom was going to drop the boys off?"

"Hey, they'll be out here in a bit, they're finishing up something," he says, walking over to me. "Let's take a walk so you can show me what you've been up to."

I'm excited to show him some of my plans for the gardens. Honestly, I always look forward to sharing this with anyone who is willing to let me garden-dump all over them.

We walk through the main section, and I unwrap my map to show him the layout. I don't miss the way he smiles when he sees me with the map. I will admit it: yes, I am a garden geek. But to do what I want to do, I have to be organized and have a plan.

I smooth it out and say, "Okay, I'm thinking this is the main garden for our inn produce and our personal growing,"

I say as I point to the spot on the map and motion to the space in front of us.

"Then over in the back, I have half of the lot set up for a lavender garden that we can harvest to sell for soaps, flower arrangements, teas, that kind of thing. I also think we can potentially sell to other harvesters, you know, down the road, and possibly turn a pretty good profit."

Evan's eyes widen and he nods, taking all of this in as I talk.

"Then back here is where I want to set up the giving garden."

"What's that?" he asks, running his hand over his beard.

"It's a community garden that Freedom Valley residents can work on together. A place to bring people together. I have a blessing box I want to ask Pete to help me set up at the front of it where people can come and get free produce. Kind of like a food pantry for anyone that needs it. I've always dreamed of doing something like this, but I wasn't ever in the position to do it before I moved here. There's no way Bradley would have ever let me have that much contact with other people back in Mississippi. I'm excited to finally get to do this—to have plenty of food for the inn and still be able to make something special for our community."

"I love that idea." Evan nods enthusiastically. And I knew he would. Evan is big on giving back and uses the inn to help the community as much as he can. He's shown me generosity and inspired me to do it for others, as well.

"I just figure that this place has been so good to me, I want to give good back, too. Maybe do workshops someday on gardening. Even a little camp for kids or something. I don't know, I just have a lot of ideas on how to expand this and make it benefit others."

"I had no idea you had so many plans. I'm on board with everything. Whatever you need, we'll help you make it happen. We also have another housekeeper coming on part-time, so that will give you a lot more availability to work back here."

My heart warms. Evan has given me more than he'll ever know in the past year. He is the first man I have ever fully trusted, other than Mitch. He's shown me a friendship that is kind, authentic, and encouraging. He says what he means and means what he says—no hidden agendas—so a compliment like this is everything coming from him. He's been a big part of me being able to heal and finally trust anyone again.

He continues looking around in awe. "Seriously. Watching you plan this all out over the past year and seeing your hard work come to life is just amazing. You should be very proud of yourself. Honestly, there's really nothing you can't do, Mel."

My mind wanders back to that night we rode in the back of Mitch's semi all the way across the country to meet up with

Evan and begin our new life. I was terrified, exhausted, and just hoped to catch a break. I barely had the courage to hope for something good to happen, yet it did. Sometimes it just takes time for good things to happen.

Some superheroes don't wear capes. They're ordinary guys like Evan and Mitch who are just good people. And if you find people like that? Hold them close and appreciate them with everything that you've got.

"Thank you," I say. "I'm so excited, and all of this makes me so happy. I couldn't have done any of it without your support."

"This is going to be good for all of us. I can't wait," he says, looking around in amazement.

I hear a vehicle door slam and look across the field to see Ty heading toward us, his ball cap pulled low, and his hands stuffed in his front pockets. He smiles at me, and it makes my lady parts jump. I straighten up and say, "Hi, Ty."

"Hey, Mellie, Evan. Did you show her yet?" Ty says to Evan.

"No, not yet. You got them?" Evan asks.

"Show me what?" I ask hesitantly, looking back and forth between the two of them.

"I asked Ty to meet me here. We set something up for you over on the other side of the field that we think you might like."

"Okay." I smile hesitantly. "What is it?" I can't imagine

what they would bring me, but if it's a plant, I'm in. Or seeds. I could always use more seeds. The guys are constantly finding things they think I need at the garden store and surprising me, so this isn't unusual, but to see them including Ty is, so I'm intrigued.

"Let's go," Ty says, reaching for my hand.

I feel the connection instantly when my hand slides into his. I've never felt this with any man, even the one I was married to and had a child with. Ty is completely different, and it's a good feeling after what I've been through. We walk to the other side of the field and there's a new, dark green building with a sign above the door that reads, "The Golden Gable Chick Inn."

My heart fills with joy. "Oh, no way! Chickens! Who did this? You two did this?" My hand flies to my mouth. I have to keep myself from jumping up and down.

Evan nods to Ty. "It was Logan and Allie's idea. We've all wanted chickens for a while so we can have fresh eggs for the inn and bakery, but I couldn't have gotten this delivered and set up without Ty's help. And he has your starter pack of chickens in the back of his truck right now."

I run my hand over the door handle, opening it and stepping in. "Starter chickens? Oh my God," I say, looking at them, happy tears filling my eyes. "This is just... so fun. Kase and Caleb are going to love this so much."

I reach over and hug Evan, and he hugs me back. Then,

without even thinking, I reach over and hug Ty, too. His arms come around me and he squeezes me gently. I stay there for a few seconds longer, not wanting to let go but not wanting to make it awkward.

"Can we get them out?" I ask.

"Of course. Let's go get them set up."

We walk over to the back of his truck where he's got seven chickens. They're all so cute. "I've always wanted chickens! Evan! I'm so excited!" I can barely contain my enthusiasm. "Wait until Kase sees this."

"Well, about that…" Evan says. "He kind of knows. He and Caleb helped Ty put it together this morning."

"You stinkers. I had no idea you were all doing this." I grin as I reach down to see one of the chickens better. "We should name them!"

"Oh, the boys have already named some of them with my mom," Evan says with an eye roll. "Just wait until you hear what they are."

"Oh my God, what?" I laugh.

"Chickira, Goldie Hen, Hen Solo, Oprah Henfrey, Lindsey Lohen, Hilary Fluff, and Hennifer." Evan says all of this with a straight face, and I laugh so hard my stomach hurts.

"That's hilarious."

Ty is shaking his head, laughing too. "Classic. I'll back up my truck and we can unload them and their supplies."

"I can't believe you guys did this," I tell Evan as Ty

climbs into his truck. "This is amazing. Farm-fresh eggs and produce!"

I watch Evan and Ty work together to unload the chickens, and then they help me get their food and water set up. It's nice to see how easily Ty fits in here with all of us. If everyone else is trusting and letting him in, maybe I should think about letting him in, too. I've been spending a lot of energy fighting this, but what if I didn't? What if I could let him in, too?

CHAPTER 11

Ty

Luckily for them, I'm not
afraid of complications.

I have spent the last couple days working, sleeping, and trying to spend time around Mellie and Kase, helping where I can and trying to get to know them better. I can't explain it, but somehow it feels like they've just always been here with me.

My phone vibrates and I answer it. It's my boss at Larkin, letting me know I don't need to be in tonight. *Perfect,* I think, knowing Mellie and Kase will be here tonight, too.

I think about the way she looked at the empty fridge the

other day, and since she told me she doesn't usually get home until after dinner, I head to the local market to grab a few things for the house. I don't want her to have to want for anything. I want her and her son to be comfortable in the bunkhouse.

Before I know it, my cart is overflowing with juice boxes, cereal, snacks, ice cream, and ingredients for various meals. I even pick up another package of coffee and a box of tea, just in case. I'm guessing money may be tight for her, so I'm happy to provide plenty of supplies for them.

I stop my cart at a display of brightly colored spring flowers by the checkout lane and grab a vase. Okay, maybe I'm trying too hard, but I want her to know I'm trying to be a good guy.

The checkout lady smiles at me when I start unloading things on the belt. "How are you today?"

"No complaints, ma'am. How about you?" I drawl before I catch myself and dial my accent back. Taking the Alabama out of my voice hasn't been easy, and it still slips out every now and then.

"Did you find everything okay?" she asks as she scans my items and places them in bags. Hoping to get out of there as quickly as possible, I nod, then help her pack things up. Before I know it, I'm sliding over a stack of bills and paying.

"Thank you," she calls as I head out.

"Have a good day," I call back as I keep moving, hoping

for less conversation.

I load everything into the back of my truck, then secure the flowers in the cup holder. I slide on my sunglasses and hit the road. I think about how lonely it's been all these months. Having people to come home to, even though it's only temporary, is a nice feeling. I didn't realize how lonely I'd been until Mellie and Kase arrived.

When I pull up, she's not here yet, and I feel disappointed. I look forward to seeing them more than I should.

My arms filled with grocery bags, I manage to open the door. Nova almost tackles me, her tail flailing a mile a minute, so happy to see me. She runs outside to do her business, then follows me back into the house, sniffing everything curiously. I get everything put away and the flowers set up on the table where Mellie can see them when she walks in.

I prepare a cowboy casserole for dinner, something my momma used to make for me all the time so it makes me feel like a piece of her is here. I realize it's been a few days since I've called her, so I pull up her number.

Her big, cheerful accent booms through the speaker. "Is that my boy?"

"It's me, Momma. How are you?" I warm inside just hearing her voice.

"Doing just fine, sweetheart. How about you?"

"Making your cowboy casserole and wanted to check in

on you and Dad." I slide the casserole pan into the oven and set the timer.

"I just got home from work, and your dad I expect is probably on his way home now."

"That's good. Anything new?"

"Nope, just that horrible woman Loraine is finally retiring." I remember her saying one of the ladies at the school district office where she works had been giving her grief for some time.

"That's a relief for you," I say.

She changes the subject. "When are you coming home?"

"Can't say for sure yet." She knows I can't talk much about my job, despite how much she wants to know more.

"Think we could come and visit?" she asks hopefully.

"No, you can't come here, but we could meet somewhere. Or I could try to come back for a weekend."

"That would be good. We miss you."

"I miss you, too."

"You tell me where and when, and we'll be there." Her usual cheerful voice has a beat of sadness to it. My gut drops. I miss her so much.

"Love you, honey. Talk soon. Bye."

We disconnect and I tidy up the cabin. I take the casserole out of the oven and let it set on the stovetop while I feed Nova and give her more water and she licks my face. "Yes, I know you're hungry. You're a good girl, aren't you?"

She eats her food while I make a plate for myself and sit at the table alone. I look around at the other chairs and think about how it might feel to come home to a wife and kids, to eat with them and hear about everyone's days. I'm working on getting to a place in my life where that can really happen.

I hear the buzz of Mellie's ATV pull up along with the sound of another vehicle and I pause my fork mid-air. She walks up to the house with Kase and a taller figure. I expect to see Evan or even Logan, but it's Preston. *Great.*

I'm still not sure about this guy, but from the sound of it, he's making his home here in Freedom Valley. People seem to really like him, but I don't like how much he likes Mellie. I shake my head, trying to rid myself of the jealousy. They're just friends... I hope.

The door opens and when they step inside, Mellie looks surprised to see me. "I thought you were working tonight. I'm sorry..."

"Hey," Preston says, stepping forward to shake my hand. I shake his back, probably a little too firmly.

"No, it's fine. I'm just finishing up, but I made plenty of supper if you guys want to eat." I motion to the casserole on the stove.

"We already ate but thank you. It smells fantastic," Mellie says. "Preston was going to help me with some things, but we can do it another time. We won't get in your way." She glances over at Preston.

"No, no worries. I ended up not having a shift tonight, but you guys go ahead and do whatever you need to do."

I don't want to intrude on whatever they're doing, but I'll admit I'm curious. Preston's a lawyer, and this looks like it goes beyond gardening and working at the inn.

I look to the little boy and say, "Hey, Kase, I was wondering if you'd like to give Nova her treat and throw her ball outside with me?"

"Sure!" he says excitedly as he takes off toward the door.

"Okay, let's go play so your mom and Preston can have a visit."

Mellie looks at me gratefully. "Thank you. You don't have to do that." She nods to Kase. "Go ahead, buddy. Have fun with Nova and Ty."

I set my empty plate in the sink and meet Kase outside.

"Alright, here's her treat," I say, leaning down to Kase and Nova's level. "Which one should we give her?"

"That one," Kase says, pointing to the milk bone.

"Good choice. Now let's make her do a trick, okay?"

Kase eagerly nods his head.

"Nova, beg," I say. Nova sits and puts her paws up then tilts her head with sad eyes. This gets a laugh out of Kase and a smile from me. "Good job. Now give her the cookie."

His little hand reaches out and before she takes it, Nova sticks her head out and swipes a big kiss up his cheek. She then gently takes the treat from his small hand. Good girl.

Kase giggles and turns to me, blinking.

"She's pretty cool, huh?"

"Yeah, she's nice, like Chip and Bossy. They can't do that trick, though. Does she ever bite people?"

"She only bites bad guys," I say, trying to be serious. "She is very protective of the people she loves. She has an important job here."

"What's her job?" he asks, his eyes widening.

"To be a best friend dog. She'll always protect you and keep you safe when you're with her. Do you need a best friend?"

He nods sadly. "I used to have a best friend dog. Her name was Sassy, but she can't be my best friend anymore." The way his voice cracks a little punches me in the gut.

"What happened to Sassy?"

"We had to leave her when we ran away with Mr. Mitch. But my mom says we're not supposed to talk about that anymore."

Whoa. This is a piece of the puzzle I wasn't expecting. Who is Mr. Mitch?

"I'm sorry about that, Kase. Maybe you can let Nova do her job and be your best friend dog. She really likes you, and I think you being here makes her very happy."

He thinks for a moment then says, "Can I have a job, too?"

I tilt my head at him. "Do you want a job?"

"Yeah. What can I do?"

"What if your job is to be a good boy for your momma and do everything she asks?"

He tilts his head back and groans. "Ugh, I already do that. Any other jobs?"

"Well," I say, scratching my beard. "What if you fed Nova every day? She needs to be fed two times per day—morning and night. It's a very important job because sometimes I'm at work. Can you do it?"

"Yes, I can. Evan lets me feed Bossy and Chip sometimes, too. And now I get to help feed the chickens and look for when they lay their eggs."

"Oh, good. So you have experience. Just what I like to hear. Do we have a deal?" I ask, sticking out my hand.

He flinches for a moment and my heart drops. *Shit.* I swear if I ever find that guy... My blood feels like it's starting to boil, but I smile through it and kneel to get to his level.

"Hey, Kase. Nova's going to keep you safe, okay?" I say with a smile and a little bit of distance between us.

He looks down but nods.

"You okay?"

"He used to hurt us."

"Who hurt you?"

"Momma said I'm not supposed to say."

"Well, I think you should always listen to your momma. But if you ever need an extra best friend, I'm here, too, okay?"

"You won't hurt us?" His eyes look up bravely as he asks this.

"Never, buddy. I'm a protector."

"Like a cop?" he whispers, looking at me with fear in his eyes.

"Yeah, kind of like the police." I try to smile. This kid is smart. Only what he says and does next shocks me more than I could have ever expected.

His eyes get bigger, and he takes a step back. "Police don't keep you safe. They lie and hurt you." And with that, he runs off to throw the ball to Nova.

And that's when I know: that motherfucker was a cop.

Mellie and Preston sit across from each other at the table. I feel like we just went two steps forward, ten steps back. The pieces to this puzzle are scattered, and I'm starting to figure out that there's a lot more to this than I first realized. This might have just got a lot more complicated. Luckily for them, I'm not afraid of complications.

CHAPTER 12

Mellie

No beards for you.

"Alright, let's get started. I know we don't have a lot of time, and I want to share with you what our investigators found." Preston takes off his jacket and hangs it on the back of the chair. He motions for me to sit and join him.

"First off, do you have any evidence saved anywhere of the abuse?" He opens his leather notebook and takes out his pen, clicking it open.

"I have a flash drive with my medical records, hundreds of photos of my body, and pictures of the house where he destroyed everything, several videos of him, and screenshots of our text messages," I say, looking out the window to make sure Ty and Kase aren't coming. I can see them kneeling in the driveway with Nova.

"That's very thorough. Wow." He looks surprised.

"I tried to get away for three years. I documented as much as I could."

"Can you get me a copy of that flash drive?"

"Yes. Evan has it for safekeeping."

"Good. That will help a lot. Okay, so I hired an investigator from out of state to go in and see what they could dig up on Bradley. And Mellie, it's really bad. Did you know he's been using and dealing cocaine and heroin?"

I sigh, partly out of relief to be done with that life and partly out of anger. "No, but that makes a lot of sense now with the way he acted and the way he always had more money than I thought we should have had on a cop's salary."

"I have enough from our investigators to bury him alone, but we want to bring everything we can to this. No stone left unturned. Got it?"

"Yes, I just know that when we do this, he'll figure out where we are and he'll come after us. We'll never be safe, and that's why we had to go no-contact when we left."

"That was probably the best decision then. The most dangerous part of an abusive relationship is the leaving. I almost always recommend my clients wait to file until after they leave."

I nod. "I tried to leave on several occasions, but it would escalate every time, and I knew that the next time I tried to leave, we might not make it." I look down at my hands, and the fear of remembering those experiences almost paralyzes me.

"We're going to be very strategic about this and make sure that doesn't happen," Preston reassures me.

"But what if he gets away with this?"

"I doubt he will with all the evidence. This is what I do, Mel. I'm damn good at it, too."

"Thank you for being willing to do this. I know it's a shit show."

It's exhausting and I wish we could just be free from him and know he'd never find us.

It's amazing to me how all these new friends of ours are so willing to help us and keep us safe, yet the one person who should have protected us, almost killed us.

After talking with Preston, I feel energized at the possibility of finally having closure, finally getting my life back.

Kase races inside, done with playing with Nova. "Can I go play in my room?" He loves having a place of his own.

"Sure, honey," I tell him. I glance back outside. Ty is standing by himself by the firepit. He runs his hand over his beard and my stomach dips, even that small mannerism making me thinking things I shouldn't.

Ty comes in just as Preston slides his notebook back into his bag and reaches for his coat.

"Ty," Preston says, nodding his head as he heads toward the door.

"Preston," Ty responds, sticking his hands in his pockets.

"Thank you again," I tell Preston as I walk him out. After talking to him, I feel hopeful that we can figure this out so I don't have to keep living in fear.

"You're sure you're good with that guy?"

I glance back at the cabin—the lights on, the green and white gingham curtains in the kitchen still drawn, the four Adirondack chairs out front around the firepit. It feels good here. He feels good. "Yeah, he's solid."

"You going to tell him about your situation?"

"Probably not. This is all temporary until the garden shed is fixed."

"He doesn't look at you like it's temporary." He chuckles.

"What do you mean?"

"That guy is so into you." Preston nods to the house.

"I'm not sure what to do with that yet."

"He seems like a good guy." He shrugs. "Maybe give him a chance."

"I'll think about it."

"Does he know that we're just friends?" I look into the

kitchen window where Ty is now pretending to do dishes in the sink.

"Nah." I grin. "I think he thinks you like me."

"Want to mess with him a little bit?" he asks.

"Maybe," I say with a devious grin.

"Give me a hug."

I walk over and he wraps his arms around me in a brotherly hug. "He *really* likes you," he murmurs into my ear. "He's dying in that window right now. You should definitely give him a chance."

"Maybe."

"Then why are we messing with him?" he asks, still holding me.

"I'll let you know when I figure it out," I reply.

"Alright, you do that." He pulls out of the hug. "Later, friend."

"Later, my dude," I say as I walk across the gravel, close the door behind me when I enter the house, and click the lock out of habit before turning on more lights.

Ty pretends to straighten the dish cloth on the sink hook. "Everything good?"

"Yeah," I say softly. "I'm just going to get Kase to bed."

"Want to hang out by the fire with me after he's down?" he asks.

His hopeful half-smile reveals a dimple that pulls me in. "I don't know…" I'm exhausted, but everything in me is begging to say yes and unwind after this long day.

"I can make you tea?"

"Alright, give me fifteen."

"Okay, I'll get it going." He pulls a mug down and turns on his kettle. *For me.* I've never had this before. Someone who just wants to spend time with me with no ulterior motive.

I head down the hall and open Kase's door, finding him sitting on the floor with all his cars out. He looks up at me mid-yawn and my heart warms. If I could go back a year and show this very scene to myself, I wouldn't have stressed and worried so much. Good things happened to us. Good things continue to happen to us.

"You ready for bed, honey?" I say, wrapping him in a hug.

"Awww, Momma. I'm not sleepy yet."

"Let's get you into your pajamas," I coax.

I hear a whimpering at the door. It nudges open and Nova shoves her way in. She jumps up on the bed and circles until she finds her perfect spot, right next to where Kase is going to sleep.

"Well, look at that. Your buddy is ready for bed. She needs you to snuggle her."

"Yeah, that's her job," he says as he pulls his pajama top on.

"Her job?"

"Ty says she's a best friend dog, and her job is to protect me and keep me safe."

My heart swells at this. "What else did he say?"

"He said I can have a job, too."

"What's your job?"

"To feed Nova in the morning and at night. She needs two scoops."

"That'll be a good job for you. Just while we're here, okay? We're going back to the garden shed when it's all fixed." I don't want him to get his hopes up that we're staying here long-term.

"Why can't we just stay here?"

"We have to stay where Evan tells us to stay."

"We can talk to Uncle Evan. He'll let us stay here," he says confidently as he reaches over to stroke Nova's head.

"Alright, let's go brush teeth. Your best friend will be waiting for you." I ruffle his hair and pull him close to me as we walk toward the bathroom.

Teeth brushed, I get him settled in next to Nova, who wiggles her little tail when he climbs into bed and gently kisses his cheek with her slobbery tongue and settles back in, I pat her head and kiss her too.

"Night, baby."

"Night, Momma."

I duck back into the bathroom and brush my own teeth quickly, running a hand through my hair. Ugh, why am I worried about how I look? It's just Ty. The guy we share the bunkhouse with. Nothing more.

I stare into the mirror, eyeing my dark roots coming in. A reminder of being Brianna in my old life. Sometimes I look in the mirror and don't even recognize myself as the new Mellie, even after a year it's still shocking sometimes. But that was the whole point. To make new identities and start fresh where we wouldn't be recognized. That doesn't mean that I don't miss myself sometimes, as weird as that sounds. I miss my old appearance, my old job, and mostly I miss who I was before I got married and everything changed. I'm not like the person I used to be at all. I'm tougher. Hardened. It's especially difficult for me to trust, to imagine having a healthy relationship with a man.

Time to dye my hair again, I make a mental note to myself. At first it was comforting to leave that nightmare behind and take on a new look and identity here in a new place. It has been exhausting, though, so if Preston can help us, we can finally breathe easier. Go back to a little bit of who we were before. The good parts anyway. I can't imagine how it could ever be the same.

I stop in my tracks as I'm walking toward the firepit. I see Ty relaxing in an Adirondack chair with a mug of tea on the seat next to him, a beer in his hand. The man really made me freaking tea to hang out by the fire. He's literally perfect.

I take a deep breath before walking toward him. He smiles when he sees me and asks, "Everything good with Kase?"

"He's asleep with Nova." I sit on the chair next to him and

he slides his arm around me, pulling me closer.

"Figures. She loves kids. Here." He reaches over and tosses me a buffalo check blanket.

I catch it and smile gratefully as I tuck it around me. "Thanks. For the tea... and everything."

He takes a sip of his beer and nods at my mug. "You bet."

I sip my tea and realize I haven't relaxed like this in the evening in a long time. It's been go, go, go for so long.

"Want some music?" He pulls out his phone.

"Yeah, what do you like to listen to?"

He thinks for a moment. "Country and rock. But mostly country."

"It's hard to be from the south and not like country. Isn't it like a requirement or something?" I tease.

He looks at me like he's trying to gauge something. "It's different up here, but I really like it. It has unexpectedly felt like home. Do you miss the south?"

I think about my hometown and realize I don't miss it at all. I have zero desire to ever go back. "No."

"Alabama and Mississippi are neighbors. Funny we were once neighbors there, and now we're neighbors here."

"Maybe we were meant to meet each other," I say without thinking.

"I told you that you'd like me," he teases.

"I told you that things with me and Kase are complicated. I don't want to put that on you."

"I meant it when I said I'm not afraid of complicated, darlin'. I think you're more afraid of it than me." He pulls me a little bit closer, like he's reassuring me.

"I am afraid," I say softly. "Kase and I consider this home for good. I don't want to mess anything up with anyone."

"You won't mess anything up." He sits back, crossing his massive arms behind his head. "When you're ready, you can tell me what you're really afraid of."

"What do you mean by that?" I ask nervously. I have to make sure my guard is still somewhat up.

"I'm not dumb, Mellie. I can tell there's something up with your past—probably something to do with your ex—and I figure when you're ready to let me in, you will. Just know that when you do, I'll be here."

My mouth drops open and then closes again. I can't figure out why he's not even the least bit bothered by the fact that "complication" is my middle name.

"What are you thinking?" He rests his arms on his legs, looking over at me.

I cock my head as I gaze at him, and I decide to be honest. "You're so ridiculously good looking, it should be illegal. And the way you can read me like a book is kind of scary."

When I met Bradley in my last year of college, he wooed me hardcore—flowers, gifts, dinners, excessive compliments. I felt like he was the love of my life. We got married right after I turned twenty-one, and on our wedding night, it all changed. The ink was barely dry on our marriage certificate before he began to show me who he really was. I thought it would get better, but it never did.

Looking back, I'm angry at myself. I realize now that I should never have stayed, but I was young, and we were married, and we had Kase fairly quickly. I couldn't just leave, and every year that I stayed he made it harder and harder to go. I became weaker, more broken down until I barely recognized myself at the end.

I know now that I didn't do anything wrong. It's just unfortunate that it took me getting away and being in a safe space to finally see it all for what it truly was.

Being with Ty... The passion, the attraction, the desire... It's all there with him. It was never like this with Bradley.

Ty laughs, bringing me back to the present, and I realize I don't hear his laugh nearly enough. He's caring, sensitive, and kind—and I get to live with him. There's a God, and right now, I believe he loves me.

"Well then, darlin', you better arrest me if I'm being illegal," he drawls, that sexy southern accent pouring through.

My stomach turns a little at the thought of cops.

"I don't trust cops."

His face falls before he calmly nods. "He was a cop, wasn't he?"

I think about what to say, the idea of letting him in both

scary and relieving. I have spent the past year keeping it all locked away like a dirty little secret, but I'm tired of running and hiding things. It's nothing to be ashamed of when I did nothing wrong.

Deciding to tell him the truth, I finally say, "Yeah."

"You want to talk about it?" he says softly.

"Only Evan and Preston know. We thought it was best when I came here that we didn't tell anyone else."

His hand takes mine and he squeezes it gently. Somehow the small gesture makes me feel safe, so I take a deep breath and I share my story.

"About a year ago, my neighbor from across the street, Mitch, helped Kase and I get out. Mitch and Evan were Marine buddies, which is why he brought us to the inn. Mellie and Kase aren't even our real names, but my ex-husband... He's extremely abusive, manipulative, and dangerous. We were married for five years, but he's a police officer, and it was hard to leave. When we finally got away, we had to go no-contact."

His face hardens and then softens a bit as he listens to me, but he doesn't react much otherwise, almost like he guessed something similar already.

"I'm sorry, Mellie. You didn't deserve any of that. I'm glad you got out, and that you had someone there to help you."

"Thanks. I shouldn't be telling you any of this, but honestly, I feel terrible not telling you if we are going to be staying here, just in case something were to happen."

"Darlin', nothing is going to happen while you live here with me. Period." He doesn't break eye contact, his gaze full of conviction and heat and honesty.

My heart softens and I almost sigh with relief.

"And Preston is helping you?"

I nod. "Preston is going to help me file for divorce and get everything straightened out so we can be here legally and Kase can start school next year. We don't even exist on paper, and we can't live on the run forever."

"I get that."

"He's scary, Ty. He has repeatedly threatened to kill both of us. I always felt like him saying it was halfway to doing it, so we had to get out. We couldn't just walk away; we had to run." My voice catches, and he tightens his grip on my hand.

"It didn't start out bad. Up until our wedding, he was fine. He was almost too nice. Then, on the night of our wedding, he slapped me as soon as we got back to our hotel because he said I danced like a slut at our reception and embarrassed him. I spent the night locked in the bathroom on the floor, crying while he slept it off peacefully, not even caring that I was hurt and devastated, or that our wedding night was ruined. I made excuses and blamed myself for everything."

Something in Ty's eyes darkens when I tell him this, and he shakes his head slightly. "Do you think he'll ever find you guys up here?"

I'd love to think he couldn't, but honestly, I wouldn't put anything past him. He's awful, but he's smart. The manipulation tactics he used were scary enough for me to never underestimate Bradley and what he's capable of doing. I have to hope that we did all we could to cover our tracks.

"We're very careful, and we will continue to be, but when I file for divorce and sole custody, that is when things will get bad. Preston is figuring it all out. That's what he was working on with me tonight."

"I'm glad he's helping you." His kind blue eyes lock on mine.

"Thanks," I whisper and lay my head on his shoulder. "It's so complicated because as a cop, Bradley has access to resources to use against us when we do file charges. I'm really scared about how things will go."

"I know you like to remind me that you can keep yourselves safe, but I'll never let anything happen to you or Kase. I promise." He says this softly, rocking back and forth on the Adirondack chair glider.

I nod. "Okay."

"I'm glad you're here at the inn."

We sit in silence for a while, but I can feel he's upset by what I just told him. It's disturbing to know this stuff when you care about someone, and I feel like he cares about us. The problem with that is that I really care about him, too. I just don't know what to do about it. Not yet at least.

CHAPTER 13

~

Mellie

I get to come home to him.

"Kase! Come on, buddy. We're going to be late!" I grab my bag and look for my shoes by the back door, where I know I placed them last night. I wonder if Nova did something with them. She hasn't bothered any of our shoes before, but they're gone, and I don't have time for this. I have a ton of rooms to clean today for fast turnarounds and Kase needs to eat breakfast. I sigh and turn around to see Nova is sitting there, watching me.

"Well?" I ask her, hands on my hips. "Have you seen our shoes?"

She tilts her head and her ears tilt back, almost like she's saying she didn't do it. She lays her head down between her paws and continues to watch me search. Finally, I step out on to the porch and there my ratty sneakers are, right next to a pair of bright red Hunter boots. A pair of olive-green Hunter boots in Kase's size sit next to his little blue sneakers.

Ty.

I snap a picture of the boots and send them to our group text.

Mellie: Look what Ty got us. You guys! I can't with this guy! (Heart eye emoji)

Beth: This is the sweetest thing!

Allie: When are you going to jump his bones?

Mellie: Eyeroll emoji.

At first, I thought kissing him was too risky, and then I couldn't imagine telling him the truth about our past, and yet I did, and he didn't freak out. He was calm and encouraging. I could tell he was upset hearing it, but it was because of *what* I told him, not because I told him at all. It felt good opening up to him, his heart is so big and he is so unbelievably kind.

I finally get Kase's new boots on and tuck his shoes into the ATV for later when we work in the garden. Before we head out, Ty pulls in and parks next to me. He turns off his truck and heads toward me. He's wearing his navy coveralls, and he looks like a manly, blue-collar man that I want to drag inside and find out what's going on underneath. Explore the tattoos that I know are there. And by the way he's looking at me, I think he just might be thinking some of the same things about me, too.

"Heading out?" He smiles and waves at Kase, who cheerfully waves back, grinning and kicking his little feet in his seat.

"Yeah. Thanks for the boots," I say, wrapping my arms around him and pulling him close.

His eyes light up and he slides his arms back around me and pulls me in for a kiss. He holds me for a minute, and he smells like leather, oil, gasoline, and woodsy spice, even after a twelve-hour shift. When he pulls back, he watches my mouth then kisses me one more time.

"I like that," he says.

"I've decided I do, too."

"Do you now?" he says, towing me over to the side of the car and caging me in with his arms on either side of me.

"Maybe." I smirk as he leans in and kisses me again. "See you tonight, Ty," I call over my shoulder as I turn around to get in the car. I chance one more look as we drive away, finding him still watching me, and he waves.

I get to come home to him.

My rooms take longer than usual to clean because I can't stop my mind from wandering to Ty. I keep waiting for the mask to fall like it did with Bradley. But it's not there. Ty is just... Ty. He just keeps getting better and better and I'm not even sure how that's possible at this point. He's thoughtful, kind, and he thinks about us and wants to be around us. And he kisses me like he means it. And I mean *means* it.

After my rooms are done, I head out to the gardens with Kase. I've set up a little makeshift place for him inside the greenhouse where I keep a couple of chairs, a cooler with snacks and water, a basket of toys for him, and his little bike that he's worn a path around the gardens with. He seems to be loving it, and when I watch him play, I know that this life suits us.

I can still remember the day Mitch told us that he'd help us. That was when I knew for the first time in a long time that everything was going to be okay. Kase was staring out the window when he whined, "Momma, I want to go outside to play." He didn't understand why he couldn't go outside like a normal kid, but nothing about our life was normal. I wanted so badly to sit out there with him and feel the sun on our faces.

"Hi, Mr. Mitch," I heard him call out the open window to the neighbor working on his pickup truck in his driveway across the street.

Mitch wiped his hands on a red grease rag and dropped it

on the top of his engine. He then walked across the lawn to the window and said, "Hey, buddy, how are you?"

"I have a truck, too," Kase said, proudly pressing his truck up against the window screen.

"Why don't I see you riding your little bike anymore?" Mitch asked.

"My daddy says we're not allowed outside anymore."

I wanted to stop him from talking and to tell Mitch to go back home. I wanted to shut the window and hide, but I couldn't help but wonder if Mitch could help us.

"Where's your momma?" Mitch asked.

I joined Kase at the window. "Hi, Mitch," I said softly, then told my son, "Baby, go get your big truck out of your toy box upstairs, okay? Let's show Mitch your big blue one."

Once he was out of earshot, I leaned in, knowing we didn't have much time.

"Can you help us?"

"I'm going to be making a long-haul trip up north in a few weeks. I think I can make a few people disappear."

"I have no money, nothing saved," I told him. "We can't leave the house anymore. He monitors everything."

"You don't need anything. Got a friend up there who could get you a job and keep you safe. Both of you."

I nod, fearful but hopeful. "Thank you," I told him, choking up, tears spilling down my cheeks, burning as they hit fresh cuts on my lip.

"Hold tight, honey. I'm going to get you out."

He turned and whistled as he walked back across the lawn, just as Bradley pulled up out front. Bradley got out of his truck and slammed the door. He approached Mitch, who calmly lied. "I dropped off some mail I got of y'alls. Y'all doing good? Haven't see y'all out and about for a minute."

Mitch played it well and it seemed like Bradley believed him.

Then Bradley came inside, slamming the door shut, "Been talking to the neighbor, I see. Whoring yourself out again."

I sink to the floor and shake my head.

"I'm sick of your shit, Brianna. Where's my fucking dinner?" He kicked his boots off and left them in the middle of the floor, ignoring his son who cowered on the stairs, looking like he was afraid to move. I jumped as I heard him undo the Velcro on his tactical vest and the thunk of that falling to the floor as well.

We have a way out, was all I could focus on. We were going to get out. I had no idea how it was going to work, but we finally had a chance.

I let out a breath at the memory of that horrible day. Of those horrible times. Life is good now. It's hard to breathe and remember that life *can* be good, but we deserve to. We deserve these good things here in Freedom Valley.

I keep daydreaming about Ty as I work in the dirt. What would it be like to be with him? Be a family? Have dinners, hold hands, take trips together, ride his motorcycle with him, build a life together, kiss him anytime I wanted to... sleep with him in his bed. Have his baby. And never ever live in fear again. What would that be like? A dream, that's for sure. I thought that life couldn't get any better than this, but it somehow has.

"Momma, I'm hungry," Kase interrupts my thoughts.

"Did you eat all of your snacks I packed?"

He nods. "When can we go home?"

"Let me finish up this row and we'll pack up. Can you put your bike and toys away?"

He pushes his bike into the greenhouse as I wipe the dirt onto my jeans and tuck my gloves into the back pocket of my pants. I breathe in the lavender and thyme in the air.

"Let's go home, buddy." I tousle his hair as we walk to the bunkhouse.

Home. I like the sound of that.

CHAPTER 14

Ty

Waiting on you.

Shit. I'm in deep here. When she explained that her ex was a cop, I was careful with how I reacted, but it's hard. I like her and her son, and for the first time since I've been on this assignment, I don't feel alone, but I don't want to lie to her.

I can't jeopardize my assignment up here, but I also know that since she's on the run and her ex is looking for her, there's nowhere she's safer than with me.

I pull out my laptop and search "missing woman and boy in Mississippi" and sadly, there are a lot of hits. I scan through all the images until I find them. There she is, with dark hair, smiling with Kase, a Christmas tree in the background. They both look so different now. They may be smiling in that photo, but to the trained eye, which I happen to have, the smiles are strained. Not the carefree smiles they have in Freedom Valley.

I read the story about them. Brianna and Jase Davidson. Missing for the past year. $10,000 reward. I search for her husband and find Bradley Davidson, a local police officer in their small town of Diamond, Mississippi.

Of course I can understand why she doesn't trust cops. The problem is that when my mission's over, she's going to know what I am, and she's not going to like it.

I didn't think I'd consider staying in Freedom Valley after this assignment, but I find myself wondering daily now what it would be like. I need to figure out what I want to do: I can either sign another contract for the next three years or find a different job. With these assignments, I can't settle down. Nobody wants to be with someone who might be gone for twelve to eighteen months at a time. I love my job, but I'm thirty-one, and I want a family of my own. Plus, now that I've spent time here, I can't imagine myself anywhere other than Freedom Valley.

And the more I'm around Mellie and Kase, the harder I know it's going to be to leave them. Now that I know the truth about why she's here and what happened to them, how could I leave? I can't take her with me when I go. She can't go back to where her ex is—not even to the next state, just a few hours over.

She's going to hate me when she finds out the truth. They all will. All I can do is hope that when I can finally come clean, she'll understand.

I have to keep my head down, focus, and try not to mess anything up. I have my work cut out for me balancing all of this until it's over.

I finish getting ready for work when I hear Mellie pull in and park. I walk outside and can't help but smile as I round the ATV to unbuckle Caleb as she unbuckles Kase.

"Nova is hungry, guys. Can you feed her?"

Kase and Caleb jump down and call out, "Yes," as they run toward the bunkhouse.

"Two scoops!" I call. Then I turn my attention to Mellie. "How was your day?" I ask as I pull her toward me, then lightly boop her nose.

"Did you just boop me?" She grins.

"Yep," I say, but my eyes are fixed on her lips.

"You heading to work?" she asks, staring at my chest.

"In a little bit."

"Well?" she asks.

"Well, what?" I ask.

"Are you going to kiss me or not?"

"Waiting on you," I say as I kiss her softly, wrapping my arms around her and holding her close.

She surprises me with how bold and outgoing she is despite everything that's happened to her. Watching the real Mellie unfold is like opening a present that with every peel of the gift wrap, I anticipate her even more.

Now that the boys are in the house, I can kiss her for real.

"Ty," she moans into my mouth which only makes me kiss her even harder.

It's then I know: I'm starting to fall for her.

CHAPTER 15

Mellie

Maybe Ty needs you and Kase
as much as you need him.

After he leaves for work, the butterflies are leaving me on a high and I need to talk about it with someone. When I'm with Ty, I just feel different, more like myself, but a new me that I don't recognize. It scares me a little, but in a good way. And the best part about that amazing kiss? He was waiting for me to do it. He wants me on my time, when I'm ready. I've never experienced anything like that before. But then again, aside from Evan, no one has ever done anything nice for me like this before. Not without wanting something in return or being sorry for hurting me.

I shut the door and pull out my phone. I send a message to our group text with Allie and Beth.

Mellie: 911. I'm starting to catch feelings, ladies. I need help.

Beth: OMG. I'm on my way. I'll bring drinks. Allie, bring treats.

Allie: Finishing up at the bakery. I can be there in 30 min.

Beth: I want to hear everything!

Allie: Don't start without me!

Mellie: I won't.

After getting the boys tucked into bed with Nova, I put on shorts and a hoodie and go out to the firepit area to wait for Beth and Allie. The air is cool for a spring night after some much needed rain. I find some dry firewood off the wood pile by the pole barn and get a fire going.

I stop and survey the gardens with pride. Everything is growing so well. I'm amazed at what I've been able to do out here with a dream and a whole lot of sweat and hard work.

Beth pulls up in her SUV. When she steps out, her jacket pops open to reveal her baby bump. I remember when she first came to the inn and hid in her room writing romance novels, all timid and closed off. Then she and Evan fell in love, and now they're having a baby. I don't know if I'm ever going to have that, a love like theirs.

Being with Bradley was traumatic for me. I've never been someone to take bullying without putting up a fight, yet I found myself beaten down to almost nothing by the very person who was supposed to protect and love me. He couldn't handle me being a strong woman with opinions and dreams. He made sure there was almost nothing left of me by the end. I had to rebuild all of that here, and most of that took place out here in the gardens. That's where I worked through so much trauma and hurt to get to where I am today.

"Earth to Mellie," Beth calls.

I shake my head to come back to the here and now.

"Where were you?" she asks as she plops into one of the Adirondack chairs and reaches for one of the throw blankets over the back.

"Just thinking about when you first got here and how happy you and Evan are now," I say with a smile. "Look at you, you're having a baby!"

"We're really happy," she says, absentmindedly rubbing her belly with one hand. "It was all worth it."

"Oh, I forgot." I reach beside my chair for a thermal mug of tea and hand it to her.

"Thanks." She smiles gratefully. "I miss wine."

"You'll have it again before you know it."

Logan drops off Allie and she hops out of the car. "Hey,

ladies... I brought the wine. And a strawberry lemonade for you, Beth."

We all wave at Logan as he drives off.

"Alright, well at least I'll be well-hydrated tonight." She reaches over to take that too and grins.

"How's the bakery coming along?" I ask.

"Oh, it's fine, but we'll get to that later. We have a 911 with Ty. Now spill."

"I have to tell you guys something. And it's probably going to freak you out."

"Okay?" Allie says hesitantly.

I think about where to begin so I can tell them without freaking them out or them feeling like I wasn't honest. I think maybe I'll just tell them a little and not everything.

"Okay, I know you both know I don't talk about before I came to the inn..." I twist my hands in my lap nervously and look between the two of them.

"It's okay," Beth encourages me, reaching over and rubbing my back. "We all have our past stuff. You know I had my past that I had to work through with Evan."

I was with Beth when she went through her past trauma and grief that she'd been hanging onto when she got here to the inn. She was able to work it out, and her and Evan are so happy now. The inn has become a sanctuary for so many of us, a refuge to find a new family or, for some of us, to start over.

I'm not sure how to talk about this, but it's getting easier, so I just go for it. "I came here to get away from my abusive husband. He's very dangerous," I whisper, not even sure why I'm trying to be quiet. I clear my throat before continuing, "He hurt us, mostly me, repeatedly, and kept us locked in our house. Evan's friend happened to be our neighbor, and he got us out by linking us up with Evan, and then Evan brought us here to the inn."

Their faces are a mix of shock and horror as I continue, "Mellie and Kase aren't our real names. I'm on the run, and we're considered missing people."

"Holy shit," Allie says, her eyes wide.

"I'm glad you're here and safe," Beth says. She's not as freaked out as I thought she would be, so I am betting Evan has told her some of the story.

"Did Evan ever tell you?"

"Not really. I only knew something had happened, and that he was keeping you safe."

"Yeah, he's really the best," I say with a sad smile.

"He really is. He loves you both so much. We all do, Mellie. No matter where you came from or what happened, you belong here with us now. We're family."

Now I'm wiping a tear from my eye and taking a deep breath.

"Hold up. Where's this asshole now?" Allie says angrily. "He needs to be dealt with."

"He's still in Mississippi. He's a dirty cop who uses and deals drugs on the side."

Allie shakes her head angrily. "What a prick."

"I told Ty." I put my face in my hands. "I really like him."

"I think he really likes you, too," Beth hedges. "Would that be so bad?"

"I mean... yeah. I can't...That's just not for me. I thought I was happy with it just being me and Kase, but everything has changed." I reach for one of the blankets on the back of the chair and pull it around me, needing the comfort.

Allie pours two glasses of wine and hands me one. I reach over and take a sip, grateful for the distraction.

"Look, Mellie, the fact that you let him in and told him why you're here? That's huge. You felt safe enough to do that for a reason," Beth says.

"I'm trying to open up more." He's become a safe space for me, and a place that both thrills me and scares me at the idea of becoming more with him.

"I just want to make sure you know that we've all got your back, whatever you need. No matter what," Allie says. "And if you need us to take a little trip and throw him off a cliff, well... I'd be open to that." She teases with the last part.

I nod and grin. "I know. And I love you guys."

"I don't blame you for kissing him. I'd climb that guy like a freaking tree if I were you." Allie sighs dreamily, breaking up the seriousness of our conversation.

The sip of wine I just took nearly goes up my nose when she says this. I wipe my mouth and laugh gratefully for the lighter topic. "I kinda want to do that, too."

"Well, what are you waiting for?" Beth asks.

"I don't know. I'm nervous." I shrug.

"What are you going to do about it?" Allie asks.

"Nothing. What if this was a mistake? This is why I need you guys to help me fix this. We should just be friends. If I start something with him, it just makes everything even more complicated."

"Start something? Honey, it's already started. You're in the shopping cart pending now. It's begun. I don't think you could stop kissing him if you tried," Allie says.

I laugh a little at the shopping cart analogy, but I know it's true. I want to kiss him again. I want to hug him, feel his arms around me. That's the truth. But do I deserve this life that I am living?

"What are we fixing?" Beth asks confused. "There's nothing broken here. You're single. He's single. Go for it. Climb that tree like a squirrel, babe."

"I don't know. Maybe we should come up with a plan. Figure out what to say and do so it doesn't happen again."

Allie laughs. "I don't know what to tell you. I think you should do it again and again and aga—"

"No! I can't do it again. I shouldn't be kissing or climbing him."

"Where's he at right now?" Beth asks, looking around.

"Work."

"Why's his truck still here?" Beth asks.

"He rode his motorcycle."

Beth fans herself. "And how does he look on that?" Her eyes cut to Allie, "I mean... I'm asking for a friend." Beth and Allie burst into laughter.

"You two are not helping." I groan and bury my face in my hands. "I'm in a pickle here." Allie opens her mouth and my eyes cut to hers. "Don't say it..." I warn, and she closes her mouth and smiles.

"You know, you could use a little fun, Mellie," Beth says. "Or with Ty, maybe a lot of fun."

"There's nothing wrong with a little kissing... or more," Beth adds.

"He's a really good kisser," I admit.

But am I good with being intimate with another man right now? What if I end up getting my heart broken again? What if I get hurt again? I trusted a man once before, and he took everything from me. He hurt me in ways I didn't think I could ever heal from. Plus, I'm still legally married.

"How did you know Logan was the one?" I ask Allie, taking the focus off me.

Allie sets her wine down and tucks her legs under her. "I didn't. He fell first. I could tell he really liked me, but just like you, I was a single mom, and I had to make sure it was a good fit for both of us. Caleb and I are a package deal, just like you and Kase."

"He fell first?" I say softly.

"Yeah. At first, he was just helping me. We come from two different worlds. He's a successful, career-driven man who had no interest in being a husband or father. I come from a family that is simple and family-oriented. But it turns out, coming from different worlds didn't mean we weren't right for each other. A love like that is a once in a lifetime, knock your socks off, love. We didn't have to force anything. We just came together because we are meant to be."

"It sounds like a fairy tale."

"There's no fairy tale about it. It was hard, too. We had to figure out how to merge these two very different worlds and make it work."

"It definitely didn't look easy," Beth says. "It was hard to watch."

"Nothing good comes easy. Sometimes you gotta work for it," Allie says. "I was on my own for years after I had Caleb, so I know how lonely it can be. Most of us aren't made to do this life alone. We need our people, and Ty seems like good people. I am thankful every day that I found Logan. He was unexpected, and he's everything I never knew we needed." She reaches over and lays her hand on mine. "The real question is, are you willing to work for it and let someone love you?"

"I don't know. I don't have anything to offer him. I'm a single mom, and I'm still a very broken person."

Beth sips her tea then adds, "You don't have to have something to offer someone in order for them to love you, Mellie. They just love you for you, the person that you are. Real love doesn't want anything in return other than love. You've come a long way since you moved here. I've seen you change a lot, even in just the last few months."

"You seem a lot happier," Allie agrees. "She's right. You are loved. Period. Logan's a millionaire. What do you think I could have offered him as an unemployed single mom? I offered him a family and love. Us. *He* needed *us*. Maybe Ty needs you and Kase as much as you need him."

"I've never thought of it like that," I say, thinking about what she's saying. "But happiness isn't everything."

"It *is* everything," Beth says. "Because life is short, and it can be gone in the blink of an eye. So treasure every moment and make the most of everything you have." Her voice is firm, but I can tell she's a little worked up.

My eyes tear up because I know she knows this all too well. Her first husband and newborn baby were killed by a drunk driver years ago, and she was still drowning in grief when she first came to the inn. It took Evan a long time to convince her that she could be happy here. It's easy to look at where people are now and forget about all the hard work it took them to get here.

"I'm sorry," I say, trying to convey understanding with my eyes. She smiles and grabs my hand, squeezing it.

"We just have to live in every moment, you know?" she says. "Do the best we can with what we've got. Don't try to figure everything out. Just go with the flow. You want to kiss Ty? Do it. If not, just chill. It'll all work out. But life is so short, Mellie. *So* short."

"Yeah, you're right. I need to stop overthinking it."

"Yeah. God, I'm tired," Allie says. "I'm going to call Logan to come get us now. Thanks for offering to keep Caleb tonight, but I think we're just going to head home and get some sleep."

She pulls out her phone and texts Logan. "He says he'll be over in five. So, what's the plan with Ty?"

"Just chill," I say with a shrug. "Just enjoy this season, get my gardens going, see what happens."

"See what happens." Beth nods in agreement. "Trust your heart."

"Alright, I'll try. We'll see," I say with a deep breath, relieved to get some of this off my chest for once.

"I'm tired, too. I'm going to head home." Beth yawns as she looks at her phone.

"Thanks for coming out, guys. We need to do this more often."

"Anytime, and yes we do." Beth smiles as she heads to her SUV and waves goodbye.

Logan pulls up and gets out of the car, kissing Allie on the cheek. "Where's our boy?"

"He's inside with Kase, sleeping. You sure you don't just want to come get him tomorrow?"

"Nah, I'll just grab him, and we'll head out so we can have some much needed family time tomorrow. Thanks for watching him tonight, Mellie."

Allie heads over to the waiting SUV and opens the door when Logan comes out carrying Caleb. He buckles him in his seat and then turns around to me after he shuts the door.

"That dog loves your kid," he says.

"We love her, too."

"I bet you sleep soundly with Nova looking out for you both," he says with a grin.

He has no idea.

"Yeah, we watch her at night while Ty works."

"Everything good with Ty?" he asks.

"Yeah, he's been nice," I reply, not wanting to say more.

"I heard the garden shed is close to being done. It's looking good."

I nod, not sure what to say. I honestly don't want to move back.

"Good, alright, get some sleep. We'll see ya." He holds Allie's door for her and then walks around and gets into the driver seat.

"Bye," Allie calls out the window.

I head inside and check in on Kase and Nova. They're curled up next to each other, his little arm draped around her, and they're sleeping peacefully. I sigh, remembering Sassy and hoping she's okay.

I'm afraid we both might be disappointed when the time does come to go back to the garden shed and leave Ty and Nova.

But what if we didn't... What if we lived here and were a family? What would it be like for Ty to come home to us every day? Me in his bed, being able to kiss him and be with him anytime we wanted?

I get ready for bed and lie there thinking about all the things that I need to do for my garden and farmers' market preparation. Tomorrow I'm going to work hard on getting everything organized. That will keep me busy and keep me from kissing Ty. Hopefully.

CHAPTER 16

Ty

They matter to me.

It's hard to focus during my shift. It's monotonous work, but it's all part of the job. I make an appearance at the factory every so often to make it look like I'm actually working here. My job is to keep a low profile and have a physical presence on occasion.

When I finish, I head home and am surprised Mellie's ATV is still there. Usually she's already over at the inn, getting started on her work for the day.

Excited that I get to see them, I unlock the door and step inside. It's already after eight and still quiet. I don't see them when I walk in, so I head to my room and take a shower, then put on sweatpants and a t-shirt. When I come out, Kase is running down the hallway, looking upset.

I kneel. "What's wrong, buddy?"

"Momma's sick," he says.

"Where is she?"

"On the bathroom floor. She won't move."

I jog down the hall and gently push open the door. Mellie's there, pale and curled up in front of the toilet.

I feel her forehead. She's burning up. "Come on, let's get you to bed," I tell her.

"No. I'm just going to die right here," she murmurs.

"You're not going to die." I pick her up and carry her into her room. I lay her down, tucking her blankets up around her.

I grab the trash can from the bathroom and set it on the floor next to her bed. Then I grab a washcloth from the bathroom and run it under cold water before ringing it out and laying it across her forehead.

I turn the light off and she tries to sit up but can't quite make it. "No! Don't shut the light off. Don't make it dark," she says desperately.

I turn the lamp on next to her bed and she moans and curls up again, drifting back to sleep right away.

I let Nova outside and when I come back, Kase is putting scoops of food in her bowl. I smile at him remembering and taking good care of her. "Hey, good job, Kase."

"I'm hungry, Mister Ty."

"What do you want?" I say as I scan the kitchen for options.

"Cereal," he says as he pads back over to his cars on the coffee table.

I pour him a bowl and set it down on the coffee table. He eats it and watches his cartoons for a moment before looking up at me worriedly. "Is Momma okay?"

"Yeah, she just needs a little bit of rest. We'll take good care of her, okay?"

He nods and continues to eat his cereal as he stares at the TV.

When I go check on Mellie again, she's still asleep and doesn't look like she's moved. She's probably caught something and is exhausted. I don't know very many people who work as hard as she does.

I send a text to Evan that she's down and they're fine at the cabin. Without waiting for a reply, I decide to try to get some sleep.

I'm exhausted, having been up over twenty-four hours, so I grab a pillow and blanket and lie down on the couch. I check the doors and make sure they're locked. "Kase, I'm going to lie down. If you need something, wake me up and not your mom, okay? Let's let her sleep."

"Are you sick, too?" he peers at me sadly.

"No, I'm fine. Just going to rest a little here." I yawn, not able to make much more sense than that.

I nap a little on and off, jerking awake to check on Kase and Mellie every so often. Once when I wake up, Kase is lying by my side with Nova tucked in at his feet. I tuck him in closer with my arm around him. I snooze some more and wake up to a patting on my arm.

"Mister Ty. I'm hungry," he whispers.

"Okay, what do you want to eat?" I mumble as I sit up.

"Macaroni," he whispers again. "Please."

"Okay," I say as I stand up and get a pot of water to boil. I let Nova out again and check on Mellie. Still sleeping. Her phone is lit up full of messages on the table next to her. I check it, realizing everyone at the inn is probably worried about her. Someone needs to know she's okay.

Messages from Evan, concerned about how she's feeling. Beth asking if she needs anything. Margie asking if she needs to come get Kase. Sasha asking what she wants to eat. These people love her, and I'm happy that she has them. And I want this, too... I want people to want to check in on me, too.

I finish making Kase's macaroni and cheese and set his bowl at the table. I pour him some milk and call out to him from where he's watching tv, his head rested on Nova's back. "Kase, your food is ready."

He comes over, Nova on his heels, and sits at the table. She curls up at his feet.

A knock at the back door makes Kase jump. I lay my hand on his shoulder seeing Evan through the window. "It's okay. It's just Evan."

His eyes light up as I open the door and Evan comes in. "Hey," I say as he wipes his feet on the rug.

"Hey, bud, how are you feeling?" he says, putting his hand on Kase's head. "You're a little warm, too."

"Is he? He wasn't earlier. How are you feeling?" I look at him and kneel down to feel his head, too. "Hmm, I'll go try to find a thermometer."

I find one in the hall closet and take his temperature, finding that it's 100.3 degrees. "Yep, you have a fever, too."

Evan looks over at me and asks, "Where is she?"

"That way." I point down toward their rooms.

Evan heads down the hall and I hear him speaking softly to her. A little while later, he comes down back. "If they get worse, call me."

I nod. "Will do."

"I can come back and drop off anything they need. I don't want Beth here. I don't want her to catch anything being pregnant and all."

"It's fine, really. I'm off tonight. I'll be around," I assure him.

He eyes me warily. "Okay. I'll check back in later. Thanks for taking care of them."

I nod, not sure what to say. I'm tired, and I get that he's

playing the protective big brother, but they're fine here.

Kase yawns at the table and I see he only ate a few bites of his food.

"Ready to go lie down with Nova again?" I ask him.

He nods and I make him a cozy little place on the sectional. Nova curls up at his side and they both fall fast asleep.

I take this time to get some sleep, too, but then wake to words no grown-up wants to hear.

"Mister Ty, I frowed up."

"What does frowed up mean?" I mumble, forgetting where I am. Before he can respond, my eyes fly open. "What? No."

I shoot up from the couch and Kase is standing there next to a puddle of what he just referred to as "frow up."

"It's okay. Let's go get you cleaned up." Nova huddles in the corner, looking at us with her ears back in an expression of concern and disgust.

"Yeah, me too, Nova. Same." I'm not going to lie, it's disgusting. I've never had to take care of a kid throwing up.

I get him cleaned up and dressed in clean pajamas, cover the couch with a blanket to protect it, and then get him set up in the living room again. Then I tackle the mess.

I look at my phone to find Evan has checked in again via text.

Evan: Checking in to see how everyone is doing.

Ty: She's still out. Kase is down now too.

Evan: Pete will drop off soup from Sasha and electrolyte drinks on the porch. He's grabbing some children's Tylenol from Allie.

Ty: Thanks, man. I'll keep you updated.

Evan: No problem.

I throw in some laundry while I wait for Pete to get here. Soon enough, there's a soft knock at the door. I open it to find Pete standing off the porch.

"How's it going?" I ask.

"How's it going with you?"

"Been better. Might not want to come near us. We're dropping like flies here," I say as I feel my own stomach rumble. Not sure if it's from cleaning up kid puke or if I'm getting sick as well.

"I can't remember a time Mellie's been sick since she's been with us. Anyway, here's some soup, drinks, and ibuprofen."

"Kase is sick now, too. They must have a virus or something."

"Hope you don't get it."

"Yeah, I'll be fine."

"Alright, take care," he says as he heads out.

"Appreciate it." I shut the door and look around.

I make a mug of soup and bring it along with the ibuprofen to Mellie. She stirs when I walk in and her eyes open. "Where's Kase?"

"He's napping on the couch." I skip the part that he threw

up because I want her to get as much rest as she can. "Pete came by and brought some soup. Also, take this," I say, handing her a few Ibuprofens.

"Thank you," she says, struggling to sit up. "I feel like I got hit by a truck."

"Just get some rest. Nova's watching over him. He's all set. Do you want the light still on?" I ask, confused as to why she hasn't wanted it dark.

"I have to be able to see if he comes back to hurt me," she says drowsy, then drifts back to sleep.

Holy shit.

She's scared of the dark because of him. I swear to God, if I ever see that motherfucker, I'm calling up my old friend Brandon down in Mississippi and we're going to take him on a little drive to Catfish Bayou and feed him to the alligators, piece by piece. What he's done to them is unforgivable. He needs to pay. No one should have to live in fear like this.

I go back to the couch and fall asleep again for what feels like twenty minutes. I wake up to a splitting headache, and I moan when nausea rolls over me. A cold hand lays on my forehead and I open an eye to see Mellie leaning over me.

"How are you feeling?" I mumble, trying to sit up to help her.

"No, lie back down. It's my turn to take care of you now," she says softly, laying a cold washcloth on my head and cheeks. It feels so good, I quickly drift back to sleep.

When I sleep, I dream about Mellie. We live here together. It's Christmas time and we're a family. The family I've always wanted and dreamed of. And the dream is nice until I wake up and realize it's still just me and Nova. She's not really mine, and I'm not sure that she ever truly can be. A pang of sadness passes through me.

I sit up slowly and look around, seeing the clock on the microwave reads 11:56 p.m. Somehow, I've slept all day, yet I'm still so exhausted.

I see the bottle of ibuprofen on the counter and take some before going to check on Kase, finding him fast asleep with Nova.

I knock softly on Mellie's door because a soft light from her lamp is still on. She opens it and she gives me a little smile. "How are you feeling?"

"I'll be fine. How are *you* feeling?" I ask, leaning against the door frame.

"Better. Thanks for taking care of us. I'm sorry about—"

I hold my hand up. "Don't apologize. We help each other. Okay?"

"Okay," she says softly.

"I heard what you said about the dark. Do you always sleep with the lights on?"

She puts her head down. "Yes, I'm sorry."

"Don't be sorry, Mel. I'm sorry that he's done this to you. You can sleep with as many lights on as you need to. I'll still be here to keep you safe, okay?"

"Okay," she whispers, her pale face looking up at me with an expression of sorrow and gratitude.

"Get some sleep," I say as I push off the frame and go to hug her. I kiss the side of her head and pull back.

"What was that for?"

"I just want you to be comfortable with me in your space, because I like being in your space. I want to kiss you, Mel," I say with a little smile.

Her face softens and she pulls me in for a longer hug. "I'm trying," she whispers.

"I know you are. Someday you'll truly understand you're safe with me." I pull her close again, feeling like we both need a hug.

This day has been a weird and long one, but I've also never felt more like a family with anyone. It takes being sick to realize that you need other people, and they need you. And it feels good to be needed and wanted. I think some people are meant to be a husband and father, and I've always felt in my bones that I am one of them.

Whatever the circumstances are, I care about Mellie and Kase now. They matter to me.

CHAPTER 17

Mellie

This is where we're meant to be.

"I see you're back among the land of the living, honey," Margie says as I walk into the kitchen in search of some much needed coffee. "How are you feeling?"

"So much better." I hug Margie.

"Make sure you take breaks and stay hydrated," Margie says in her motherly tone. "Take care of yourself."

"I will. Thanks."

"Any plans tonight?" she asks.

"Just checking in on the gardens and getting some extra rest. I'm glad no one else here got whatever we had."

"Let me know if you need any help with Kase. I could use some help emptying my cookie jar." She winks at me before going into the kitchen, not even bothering to wait for a response.

I pop in my headphones and play my audiobook as I set off to work.

I hit the jackpot with the inn. This is where we're meant to be.

I can't stop thinking about Ty all day, wondering how he's feeling and when he works next and when we can spend time with him. I really liked taking care of him, and I liked him taking care of us. I send him a text message to check in on him.

Mellie: How are you feeling?

Ty: Good, how about you guys?

Mellie: Good, just finishing up work, then I'll be home.

Mellie: I mean at the bunkhouse.

Ty: This IS your home, Mellie.

I smile hearing him say that. I like the thought of the bunkhouse being our home with him. I want to come home to his hugs and get more of our stolen kisses.

Mellie: See you tonight (Kiss emoji)

Ty: Looking forward to it.

I get to work and get everything done so I can get my gardens taken care of before heading home. This was a long day, and I finished an entire audiobook just while working. It felt good to get lost in my work and lost in my thoughts about Ty.

As I get to the garden shed, I spot Toad coming up the path toward me.

"Hey there." I smile at the biker who has a name that doesn't match his looks. He's a good-looking man, with piercing blue eyes, wild, long brown hair and matching beard, and he wears the typical leather biker cut.

"I'm great now that you're here." He smiles. I know he's not really interested in me, he's just a shameless flirt.

"Oh, Toad." I shake my head. "What are you doing here?"

"Came to see Evan about possibly hosting a biker retreat here this summer. You headed home?" he asks, nodding to the shed.

"Yeah, but I'm not living there anymore. There was a flood, so we're in the bunkhouse now, rooming with Ty Flynn. You might know him. He works over at the Larkin factory. You work there, too, don't you?"

"I know Ty Flynn, but I haven't seen him at the factory. Are you talking about Flynn who works part-time for Sam Sr.?"

"Yeah, that's him."

It seems weird that Toad hasn't seen him at work considering Larkin's not that big of a place. Maybe they work different shifts?

"Well, I better go, Toad. Evan's in his office. See you around."

I get so deep in my gardens that I realize I've lost track of time. I need to get back to the bunkhouse for Kase, who's being dropped off soon by Allie and Logan.

It's getting dark and the sun is about to set. Logan passes me in his truck, then stops and backs up. "Hey, Mel. Caleb and I had to take off. Kase and Ty are roasting marshmallows, waiting for you."

"Sounds fun. Hi, Caleb," I say, waving to him in the back seat of Logan's truck. "Thanks for dropping Kase off."

"No problem. We'll see you tomorrow."

Watching Logan become a dad has been one of the most heartwarming things imaginable. He's one of the reasons that I have hope that I can find that again someday. There are good men out there that want a family.

Like Ty.

Maybe someday the thought of being with someone won't be as terrifying as it seems. Ty does make it easier and easier every day.

I head to the side of the cabin and stop when I hear Kase and Ty talking. I pause and listen because they're so cute together and I want to hear what they say. I'm a snoop, sue me.

Kase looks up to Ty. "One more?" he asks with a mouthful of marshmallow.

Ty tilts his head as if he's weighing whether he should say yes or not. They're sitting in the Adirondack swing together, side by side. Seeing Ty's massive shoulders set next to Kase's tiny little frame is just adorable.

"Okay," he says with a grin. "But if your momma gets mad, you better give her the eyes." His southern drawl is really coming out now. He tries to keep it in, but it's really strong when he lets his guard down and is relaxed like he is right now. I wonder why he tries to hide it.

"What eyes?" Kase asks, confused.

"You know, the puppy dog eyes. Like this..." Ty makes a face I can't see.

"Does that work?" Kase asks curiously.

"Probably not on your momma, she's smart. Nothing's going to get by her," Ty replies. He lances a marshmallow onto Kase's stick.

"Can I ride your motorcycle sometime?" Kase asks, hopeful.

Ty laughs. "Your momma definitely wouldn't like that."

"Why not? She likes it when you drive it."

Ty tilts his head down at Kase. "Why do you say that?"

"Because she always watches out the window when you get on it, and she goes like this..." He exaggerates putting his hand on his chest, pretending to swoon.

Ty laughs again. "Does she now?"

"Yeah, I think she likes you even though she pretends she doesn't. She likes Nova, too. Sometimes she sneaks extra chicken for her when you're not looking." He shrugs.

"That's really nice of her."

"Nova is my best friend now."

"I love that for you, Kase."

"Do you like my mom?"

"Yeah. I like your mom. And I like you, too."

My heart is so full listening to them, even though Kase is telling my secrets. That's what little kids do—they always tell the truth and they always call you out. They see things we don't even say. I smile as I step out from behind the house and walk toward them.

"Hey, guys. Save any for me?" I call as I cross the lawn. It's cool and cozy and a perfect night for a firepit.

"Momma!" Kase says as Ty takes his stick so he can run

over to hug me.

"Did you have a good day, bug?" I kiss his head and hold him to me.

"Yeah, I've only had six marshmallows," he states proudly.

"He's had two," Ty calls as he gives me a look that makes me want to tear off my clothes and jump him as soon as I get Kase to bed. His eyes meet mine and lock in there. I swear this guy knows what I'm thinking, and when he nods with his sexy grin, I bite back a grin of my own and force myself to look away, the heat rising to my face. I'll blame it on the heat from the firepit.

"You can have mine, Momma. I can make another."

"Thanks, honey." Ty hands me the stick. His hand brushes mine as he stares right at me. Yeah, he knows what he's doing.

"You're not working tonight?"

"Nope." He pokes another marshmallow with the stick. He looks so good in his faded grey T-shirt that reveals his massive biceps and forearms. I'm standing close enough to him to detect the campfire aroma on his clothes. It's fitting, since I feel like I'm playing with fire with him.

"How was your day?"

"Pretty good." I'm still curious about what Toad said earlier, so I casually throw it out there. "Hey, I ran into Toad and asked if he knew you. He said he doesn't recall you working at Larkin. Do you know him?"

He looks at me carefully and says, "I know Toad from Sam's mostly. He works on his bike there. Sam's a club member with Toad."

"Hmm, weird. Must be a big place over at Larkin if you don't see each other all that much." I take a bite of marshmallow, thinking about what he said. It makes sense, but I still have a funny feeling about it. "Good stuff. Where's Nova?" I look around for her.

"Napping in the chair," Ty says as we look over and see her wrapped in a light blanket, snoring.

"Some guard dog you've got there."

"Oh, don't let that fool you. She saw you creeping around the corner earlier eavesdropping on our conversation and dimed you out." He shoots me a knowing wink.

I put my head down and smile, embarrassed as I put my arms around Kase and hug him close.

Ty squeezes my arm with his hand to let me know that we're good, and his touch feels light, comforting, and I want more of it.

Now I'm just feeling silly about questioning whether he really worked at Larkin or not. It's probably just my past worries creeping in.

"And how was your day?" I ask him as I sneak another glance over at his strong, square jaw hidden under his trimmed beard.

"Better now," he says softly as he inches closer to me and

wraps an arm around my waist. My skin feels hot where his hand is.

Okay, now I really am anxious to get Kase to bed so that I can have some alone time with him.

"After you finish that one, it's time for your bath and bed, okay?" I lean in and kiss Kase's head, still tucked into Ty.

"Awww, Momma..."

"After he goes down, want to sit out here with me?" he asks.

My heart feels like it skips a beat for a second, and he leans in and smiles at me knowingly again.

I look between the fire, Ty, and Kase, and my heart feels so full. We could be this. We could be a family. Maybe. It can't just be a physical connection, right? I wonder what this would even look like or mean? Can you love someone when your past is buried and your life is built on a secret? I can't fully be with him. I am still married, I have a different name, we don't even truly exist on paper. I start to feel doubt, and he must sense something because he whispers in my ear, "Stay with me, Mellie."

"Yeah," I say as I stand, shaking off the negative thoughts and focusing on the now. "Let's go get ready for bed, honey." We set our sticks down next to us. "Come on."

Reluctantly, Kase follows me inside with Nova trotting behind her new boy that she's in love with. It's funny how I fell for Ty and she fell for Kase. We do fit together, that's for sure.

"You really are a best friend dog, aren't you?" I whisper as I stroke her soft head. She kisses my hand in return and curls into Kase, now settled in bed. I lean down and kiss her head. "Thank you, Nova."

I stroke Kase's cheek for a moment, so grateful for him. "I love you. I hope you sleep well and have good dreams."

He yawns and nods. "Love you, Momma," he murmurs as his little arm curls around Nova.

I kiss his head one more time and shut his door, grabbing a hoodie on my way outside.

"I stole your hoodie," I tell him as I approach the firepit.

His mouth turns up as he stokes the fire. "You can have whatever you want from me, Mellie."

"Careful what you wish for," I murmur softly, not thinking he hears me, but his gaze turns and locks on mine, sending heat through my core.

He looks so good sitting there in the light of the fire. I realize there's so much I don't know about him and I want to get to know him more.

"Let's play a game," I say.

"I don't know if I like games," he teases, but there's a note of seriousness in his tone.

"This is a fun game. Called Get to Know Ty Better."

"What do you want to know?" he says finally, still staring into the fire.

"What's your family like?"

He relaxes with this question, and I can tell he loves his family just by the way his face lights up. "My mom works for a school district and my dad's a mechanic."

"Is that how you got into being a mechanic?"

"Something like that. I grew up fixing things with him."

"Where do they live?"

He's slow to reply and then he finally says, "They're still in Alabama."

"Do you miss them?" I ask.

"More than anything. That's the only hard part of being up here. I don't get back as often as I'd like."

"Can they come visit? I bet they could stay at the inn."

"My momma was asking about that the other day. That would be nice. I think you'd really like them, and I know they'd just love you and Kase."

"Tell me more about them." I squeeze in closer to him and rest my head on his shoulder.

"I already told you, but my momma grows the best tomatoes in the entire south. She's patient and kind, and she's a good mom."

"She sounds great. I wish she could come try the tomatoes you helped me plant."

"Yeah," he says. "And she would love that. Is there anything better than a fresh tomato sandwich?"

"I can think of a few things, but that's right up at the top of the list."

Ty hears Nova whine at the door and goes over to get her.

"How did she get out of Kase's room?"

"She opens doors."

"No way. How did she learn that? I've never met a dog that opens doors."

"Yeah, she can do the lighter interior doors, but she struggles with the heavier exterior ones."

"That's wild."

Nova relieves herself out in the yard, then comes over and snuggles up next to me on the chair. "Well, hello there," I say, rubbing her ears. "You didn't want to snuggle my boy anymore?"

He tips his chin up over at me and asks, "Where's your family?"

"My parents died in a car accident when I was a little... I hardly even remember them. I was raised by my great aunt, but after I graduated from high school, she moved on and I don't hear from her anymore. It's just me and Kase now."

"I'm sorry, Mel. That's sad."

"Yeah, well, it is what it is. The inn and all these people? They're my family now."

His eyes watch me and soften. "She likes you," he says, motioning to Nova, easing into a lighter subject.

"I love her," I say softly, petting her ears as she leans into me for more, closing her eyes. "We had a dog back home, but we had to leave her when we ran. It makes me too sad to think about her now," I say, wiping a tear quickly and kissing Nova's cheek. Ty is watching us, not moving. His expression is unreadable and he's so still it's concerning.

"What?" I ask.

"Just sad about your dog. That's not right," he finally says. "She really loves you and Kase." He looks like he wants to say more but he's not if he should.

"What about you?"

"I'm definitely also falling for you, Mel," he says without hesitating, a big smile spreading across his face.

"I'm definitely falling for you, too," I whisper, my heated gaze on his.

"What are we going to do about this?"

"Well, it's scary as hell, but let's see what happens?" I ask as I lean into him and kiss him softly.

"I can do that," he says as he folds me into his arms and pulls me onto his lap. He kisses me as his hands explore my breasts. I suck in a deep breath, wanting him to touch me, craving his hands on me. The fire light warms us as he kisses me, his hands exploring and pulling me closer, mine gripping his thick shoulders.

We both pull back after a while and his eyes are on mine. "I really love you, Mel."

"I love you, too," I say, still breathless.

"I want it to be right when we do this," he says, holding

me tight.

"What do you need for it to be right?"

Sadness creeps in, along with guilt that I can't be without the baggage that I'm carrying from my past.

He doesn't take it further, just kisses me once more for reassurance, and puts out the fire as we finally go inside.

"I want it to be perfect when we're finally together. Good night, Mellie," he whispers as he tucks me into bed and turns on the lamp, kissing me one last time before he heads to his room down the hall. My heart catches that he remembered that I wanted the light on, but I hadn't even realized they were off.

CHAPTER 18

I need her and she needs me.

I want more with her, but not until I can be fully honest about who I am and why I'm here in Freedom Valley. She deserves that, and I want what we have to be built on truths—not half-truths or whatever this is. I know I'm doing the right thing, but it doesn't mean it makes me feel good about it all. Sometimes doing the right thing doesn't feel like the right thing, but I know in my heart that this is going to work. You don't have what we have and not believe it's going to work out. Somehow, I just know it will.

I finish my shift with Sam Sr. and start to put away

my tools. Sam wraps up his own project for the day—a motorcycle he's fixing for one of his biker friends—and washes his hands in the industrial sink stained with oil and grease.

"What's up?" I ask him.

I've liked working with Sam Sr. here at the shop. He's been a good boss to me, and he's made it a hell of a lot less lonely here, especially before I met Mellie and the crew at the inn. He and his local motorcycle club, the Eastern Bones, have taken me under their wing. I'm not an official member and don't have an interest in being one, but I have become good friends with a lot of them and fixed things for them when I can. I look forward to rides with them, and I may not wear the cut they wear, but I'd consider a lot of them good friends.

"Not much. Just staying busy," he says, but he looked sidetracked when we worked together on an engine of a motorcycle we're rebuilding. I had to call him back to the job and help him focus several times, so I know something is bothering him.

"How's it going having your son home?" I say as I look up to where my old apartment was, where Sam Jr. stays now.

He runs a hand over his beard. "He's not doing well. Hasn't come down in a while. I can't seem to get through to him."

"What's going on?" I pause with concern. I know Sam Jr. came back from the military, and that he has PTSD and other things going on. Sam has been hesitant to talk about it, but

I know it's been bothering him.

"I don't know. I feel like I'm losing him." He looks worried. "I think it's just going to take some time. His last tour overseas really messed him up."

"I'm sorry to hear that, Sam." I've gone through some similar stuff on the job, and I wouldn't wish it on anyone. But, of course, I can't tell Sam this.

"Yeah. We're just trying to be here for him. He's been working at night when no one is around. I think he's having trouble sleeping and I know he wants to be alone, but now I'm wondering if that's helping."

"I'm happy to talk to him if you think it will help."

"I know. I appreciate it. I'll ask him tonight. How're things going with your new living situation?"

I run my hands under the water and wash them several times to get the grease stains off. "It's good. It's nice not coming home to an empty house, you know?"

"I know exactly what you're saying. Been coming home to an empty place for years now."

I don't know a lot about Sam Sr., but I do know he raised Sam Jr. and his sister alone as a single father. He's close with his motorcycle club, but I've never heard him talk about having a woman in his life.

We work together in silence as we close the shop for the night until Sam says, "Would you ever think about coming on here full-time? I've got a full-time opening coming up when Tony leaves at the end of summer. I know you're over at the factory, but maybe this could be an option..."

I think about it and wish it really were a possibility. The façade of the life I'm living right now with working at Larkin and then coming home to Mellie and Kase is probably not really an option. But damn if it doesn't feel like the life I want to be living. *Should* be living. If only the timing were right.

"I'll think about it. Thanks for the offer." That's all I can really say for now. We'll see how things unfold and if his offer still stands in the upcoming weeks.

"You're a damn good mechanic, Flynn."

I don't need to think about it—I want it. It would be great to work here full-time and make a life here. But unfortunately, when this assignment wraps up, I have no idea where my real job will take me. I haven't been able to be honest with Mellie or anyone else here because I can't jeopardize my assignment. When I can, I only hope they'll accept me and understand that I did what I had to do.

I pick up dinner from Freedom Pizza on the way home. Cheese for Kase and a meat lovers for Mellie and me. I smile when I pull in and see the lights on and Mellie's ATV parked out front.

They're home.

As I walk up to the front door, I can hear she's playing Zach Bryan music. As I get closer, I pause and watch her chasing a giggling Kase around the living room. She has no idea how much I want her. *Want this.* I've never felt more sure about anything. But when she knows the truth, will she still feel the same?

She causally glances at the front door and freezes when her eyes catch mine. There's a quick flash of terror in her eyes before she realizes it's just me. I set down the pizza and go to her, pulling her into a hug, making sure she knows she's safe.

"Hi, beautiful," I murmur into her hair.

She's still breathing heavily and shaking. "Hi, Ty."

"I'm sorry if I scared you."

I scan the room and see Kase peeking out from behind the couch. "Hey, Kase. It's just me. How's it going?" I try to remain calm, so I don't freak him out even more.

He slowly slides out from behind the couch and has wide eyes, watching me as he reaches for Nova and pulls her in for a hug. And damn if that doesn't warm my heart that he uses my dog for comfort.

"I brought pizza. Did you guys eat?" I rub Mellie's back and hold her to my chest until her breathing slows down.

"Not yet. I was just thinking about what to make or if we'd go over to the inn and find something," Mellie says.

I pull back and say, "Why don't you go get some plates and I'll check in here with Kase."

When she heads into the kitchen, I kneel and stroke

Nova's head, giving him space. "Hey, Kase."

"I don't like it when Momma gets scared."

"Me neither. I don't want anyone to be scared here. You don't have to worry about me. I'll never hurt you or your momma. I'm a safe space. Okay?"

He nods, looking relieved but still unsure. "Okay." It breaks my heart seeing this kid's reaction of wanting his mom to be safe. He's only four, but he's seen some hard stuff.

I'm not entirely sure where he puts everything he eats, but this kid is always hungry. He runs around all the time, though, so that probably explains why he has endless energy and a bottomless appetite. Already knowing the answer, I ask anyway, "Are you hungry? I got you cheese."

His eyes brighten a little. "I love cheese."

"Let's eat," I say as I hold out my hand and he accepts it. Relieved at his reaction, we go to the kitchen where Mellie has plates and drinks set up.

"All good?" Her eyes go over Kase holding my hand and her eyes soften as she watches us walk toward her.

"Yeah." I squeeze her shoulder gently.

"Thanks for bringing dinner. You didn't have to do that."

"Thanks for being here so I don't have to come home to an empty house."

"It's not empty. Nova's here," Kase pipes in.

I smile and make sure they have their plates of pizza before I get mine and join them.

"That's true, but she would have been here all alone," I say, pulling up a chair next to Kase at the table.

"Do you work tonight?" Mellie asks me as she sits down across from me.

"No, I'm off. I was thinking we could work on your garden after dinner if you want. I can show you some trellis stuff with your tomatoes."

Her eyes light up at that. "Really? You want to do that?"

"Yeah."

"Okay." She bites a smile on her lip. "How was your day?"

"Better now," I say, thinking about what I want to do to that lip she just bit. We'll get to that later.

My phone vibrates, and once I see it's just my dad, I silence it and slide it back into my pocket. He's probably just calling to check in, so I decide I'll call him back after dinner. But I feel it immediately buzzing with another call and look down to several texts and the screen lit up with his name again. Something is wrong.

Dad: It's your momma.

Shit.

"I'll be right back," I tell them as I go outside and answer the call. "Dad, what's wrong?"

He chokes back tears as he says, "I had to rush her to the hospital, son. I found her collapsed on the kitchen floor when I got through with work."

"Okay, I'm going to come home on the next flight that I can get on."

"Probably best, son." His voice breaks. I have never heard my dad cry or seen him this distraught.

"What are the doctors saying?"

"They think it's her heart."

My own heart drops at hearing this. Panic starts to fill me, and I shake my head and shake it off so I can focus on what I need to do.

"Okay, I'll call you as soon as I can," I say as I turn around, my eyes meeting Mellie's worried ones as she's standing in the doorway.

"What's wrong?" Her hands grip my arm and she pulls me in, her eyes searching mine.

"It's my momma. She collapsed and is in the hospital. They think it's her heart. I have to go home to her."

"Okay, why don't you go pack and I'll look up flights for you?" she offers.

"Okay, I need to fly into Mobile." I need to make so many calls, pack a bag, get a flight, and I need to it all *fast*. It's making me overwhelmed. "Find me the soonest one you can, please. I appreciate your help."

"Of course," she murmurs as she pulls out her phone and sits down at the table to begin searching.

In my room, I mindlessly throw clothes into my duffle and think about my momma. I feel bad that I'm so far from home and haven't been able to visit her much lately. And even guiltier when I couldn't let her come up here.

Kase hugs my leg as I pass and pats my thigh with his little hand. "Thanks, Kase," I say, hugging him to me. "Will you take good care of Nova?" I ask as I look over to Nova leaning into us as she licks Kase's hand.

"Yes," he says solemnly. "Are you coming back?"

"Of course I am." I tousle his hair, trying to lighten the mood. "It looks like she'll take care of you, too."

Mellie looks over at me and says, "I found one. How does this look?" She hands me her phone to look at the flight information.

My eyes scan it and I see it leaves in the next few hours. "Looks good." I grab my wallet out of my back pocket and complete the purchase.

"Want me to drive you?" she offers.

"Yeah, honey, that would be good."

"Of course," she says as she pulls me into a hug and lays her head on my chest.

This. This is what it would feel like to have her as my woman. Someone to carry you when life kicks you in the balls. I need her and she needs me.

As I wait to board my flight, I think about Mellie. I need my momma to be okay; I want her to meet them. She's been after me for years to find a nice woman to settle down with and give her grandbabies.

I check my group texts with my brothers and sister, and they're just as worried as me. We're all meeting up in Alabama.

My phone rings and I answer it, "Flynn."

"I heard you're going back home for personal reasons."

Mack, my field division superior, checks in on me often and I know he won't be pleased about me leaving during the operation just as it's heating up.

"Yeah, it's my mother. I'll touch base with you as soon as I know more."

"Okay, I'm sorry about your mother, but you need to be back here as soon as you can. We're close to finishing."

"Will do. And Mack, I also want to talk to you about my next contract. I'm not sure I want to renew." I can't even believe the words rolled off my tongue. I've always wanted to do this job, but lately, I'm rethinking everything.

"Why?" I can tell by his tone that he's surprised.

"These assignments aren't conducive to the life I want to live."

"We can talk about it later. Just finish this assignment. If you want out, I'll help you get out after this one. You're a fine agent, one of the best I've ever worked with at ATF. We'll be sad to see you go, but I understand."

"Thanks. I just wanted to let you know where my head's at."

"Just get back here as soon as you can. I hope your mom is okay. It'll work out, Flynn."

I want to build a life I can be happy with, with a woman who loves me, a family. Damn it, I want that so bad. I thought this would be a lifelong career for me, but I want other things more now. The job led me to Mellie, though, so I'll always be grateful.

I have hard choices to make, that's for sure, but for now, I have to get home.

CHAPTER 19

Mellie

I want this with him.

We miss him and he's only been gone a few days. It's crazy that in the short amount of time we've lived with him in the bunkhouse, we've become so close and intertwined in each other's lives.

I drove Ty to the airport and he told me to borrow his truck whenever I needed it, so I went ahead and ran some quick errands in town. I stop in front of Allie's new bakery, Baked Inn Love. I admire the window at the front of the bakery and smile. Watching this dream come together for Allie has been incredible to see, and I'm so excited to see the inside of the store now that she's so close to opening.

I walk up to the dark walnut double doors and peer inside. I run my fingers over the ornate wood and take in the big, picture windows with the letters beautifully etched in the glass.

The door swings open, and Allie startles me. "Get in here. We were just talking about you and all your beautiful décor that you helped me with." I grin as I head in and give her a big hug. Having them include me in their dreams and watching it all come together makes me feel even more a part of their family.

"This looks fantastic!" I take in the boho-chic vibe of the bakery. It's homey, eclectic, and stunning, with soft pinks, mint greens, wood tones, cream walls, and bright green plants lining the walls with terra cotta pots that she let me help her choose. Large, round tables with cozy oversized chairs are scattered around the front and a few sofas are set up throughout the space.

"Your plants look amazing!" I examine them all lined up on the wall.

"Thanks to you helping me figure out which ones I should choose." Allie beams as she shows off her greenery.

"Of course. I love how they turned out, especially in the planters we painted."

"It wouldn't have looked anything like this without your help, Mellie. You have an eye for decorating. Saved us a lot of money, too," Allie says earnestly. "Beth's here. She came for provisions. You hungry?" Allie calls over her shoulder as she reaches for plates and a platter of food from the fridge.

"I'm always hungry. What did you make?"

"A little bit of everything. I made the coolest charcuterie board and I want your feedback on it. I'm thinking about offering these for parties with different themes."

"Happy to help, that sounds great." I glance at the empty bakery cases that I know will be filled with treats soon, distracted by all of the beautiful fixtures and details of the soon-to-be-popular bakery. The whole town has been talking for months in anticipation of the opening.

"Okay, come back and see the kitchen. I can't wait to show you the new giant ovens Logan surprised me with. Talk about a timesaver. I can make a whole day's worth of treats at once."

We walk back through the double doors to find Beth sitting on the counter, snacking on the charcuterie board, proudly cradling her baby bump.

I say hello, then pop an olive into my mouth.

"Oh, good, you're here. We were just about to text to see if Evan would bring you by. How'd you get here?" Beth asks.

"Ty's truck."

Beth's eyes widen. "Oh, really. How are things going with you two? Spill."

"Uh-uh. First the tour, then snack and gossip. In that

order."

I scan the kitchen, taking in the modern but functional black and white tile backsplash that looks amazing with all of the natural wood elements built into the kitchen. Beth's baking supplies are lined up and organized on a counter in clear oversized baking storage jars for easy access and measuring.

"This is where all the magic is going to happen," Allie gushes. "I'm going to create family memories with custom cakes, treats, and goodies for every occasion. The upstairs will be used for events and gatherings. It's not quite finished yet, but I want to show you anyway. Logan's making us put on hard hats if we go up there." She hands us each a hat.

"Ohh, I'm going to borrow one of these for Evan. It'll go great with his tool belt," Beth says with a wicked grin.

"Eww, gross. That's my brother." Allie makes a pretend throwing up sound.

"You can share your hard hat with Logan," Beth says, sliding on her hat.

"What makes you think I already haven't?" Allie grins wickedly.

"I hope it's not the one I'm wearing."

"Speaking of hardhats and toolbelts, have you guys seen the garden shed?" I ask. "I saw that it's finished, it looks like they did a great job on it."

When Evan first showed me the completed shed, I was

nervous I'd move back right away and have to leave Ty. So far, though, no one has said anything about it, so we're just staying put. Plus, we have Nova now, and I can't imagine separating her and Kase. Heck, I can't imagine separating from Ty. I miss him so much.

"You're not moving back, are you?" Beth asks, looking worried.

"No, going to stay with Ty for now." I smile sheepishly.

"Good, because I like Ty with you. He seems good for you guys," Allie says as we start for the stairs.

We climb the wooden steps with a metal railing. We reach the top and there's a big, beautiful landing with bookcases. Allie is excited as she leads the way, and I'm thankful for a change in conversation.

"This will have seating areas spread about and side tables with cozy lamps. We were thinking about offering to host book clubs here, bridal showers, birthday parties, things like that. In the back, we have a few other rooms we're thinking of using for meetings, maybe even co-working spaces for people looking for a quiet place."

"That would be a great use of space." Beth looks around. "I love the hardwood floors and huge windows."

"Next week, right?" I ask.

"Yes, we are still on for our soft opening in a week and our grand opening in two weeks," Allie says excitedly.

"It's been so cool watching your dream come true," I say,

my chest filling with pride seeing Allie so happy.

"It smells so good. Cookies baking, freshly brewed coffee. This is going to be the hot spot of Main Street here in Freedom Valley," Beth says dreamily.

"Now let's go eat. I'm hungry, and I want to know all the things going on with you two."

"Me too." Beth follows her down the stairs.

"You're always hungry," Allie jokes.

"Yeah, well, I'm eating for three," Beth says.

We stop and turn and gape at her, seeing her mouth slightly open.

"Wait, what?" Allie and I say at the same time.

"Okay, so I tried to hold it in, but I couldn't. I have to tell someone or I'm going to explode." Beth eagerly clasps her hands together and jumps up and down on the last stair.

"Please don't do that," I say nervously, my eyes wide, looking at her belly and back to her.

"Are you telling me—" Allie begins.

"Twins!" Beth shouts. "Twins! I just found out, and I'm stress-eating because I don't know how to tell Evan. I need your help."

"He's going to lose his mind." Allie's face lights up. "He wanted a baby so bad, and now there's two? Oh, Beth..."

"I know. That's why I need you two to help me come up with a clever way to tell him." She beams.

"Isn't he coming to get you tonight?" Allie fills up water

glasses for the three of us.

"Yep, so we gotta think fast."

Allie brings the drinks to the dining area and sets them down.

"This is a lot of food." I smile with delight as I look at it all and think about how I want to dig in.

"Have you seen how much Beth eats lately?" Allie asks. "I'm still trying to figure out where my pan of cinnamon rolls went."

"They went to a *very* good place," Beth says seriously, rubbing her belly. "I wasn't the only one who demolished them. Evan and his babies helped."

"Oh my God, he's going to lose it. I can't wait to see his reaction."

"For sure, we'll do it when he comes." Beth snags a handful of nuts and grapes. "Now, tell us about Ty. What's going on?"

"Ty and I..." I realize it feels good to say that out loud. "Well, I told him I loved him."

"Did he say it back?" Allie asks.

"Yeah, he did. But then he kind of turned me down, like he didn't want to *be* with me. He said something about wanting it to be perfect."

"Wanting what to be perfect?" Beth asks.

I blow out a breath. "I don't know. That's just it. I don't know what I did wrong."

"Maybe he has something special planned for when he

gets back?" Allie says.

"Maybe." I shrug. "He's so confusing. He loves me, but he's holding back with something."

"How do you feel about everything?" Beth asks.

I think about it for a second and my heart warms. "He helped me with my gardens, and it was great, you know. He's patient. He doesn't make me feel dumb when he shows me how to do something. He's kind, and he seems to truly like being with me," I say, confused. "I mean, he's falling in love with me, and I can't for the life of me understand what he sees."

"You're a total catch, Mellie. I mean, look at you. You're the whole bag. Strong, assertive, beautiful, loving, and fun to be around. Who wouldn't want that?" Beth argues. "Don't you feel that about yourself?"

Allie looks at me dreamily. "There's nothing more attractive than a man who teaches you something without making you feel dumb. Just connecting with you and being in that moment."

"Exactly. We do have a special connection."

"What do you think is the biggest thing stopping you?" Allie asks.

"I feel like he's holding back, like there's maybe something he's not telling me. I don't know what it is or why I feel that way, but I do." I can't put my finger on it, but something feels off, and I don't know if it's me just being paranoid or what.

"Like he has a secret?" Beth asks.

I never thought about it like that. What if he's holding back something and isn't who he says he is? I don't think he would do that, but I have a weird feeling that I can't seem to shake.

"Yeah. I just don't know what."

"Any clues from around the house?" she asks.

"I'm not snooping on him."

"What? It's not snooping. It's investigating," Allie says. "Start with his underwear drawer."

"You're ridiculous," I say, and we all laugh. "You just want to see his boxers."

"Oh, so he wears boxers?" She flutters her eyelashes.

"I have no idea, creep." I throw a grape her way in mock frustration.

"Ty seems like a reasonable guy. If he's going to hide something, he'd have a good reason," Allie says. "Just talk to him."

"Yeah, like maybe he's a secret agent," Beth offers. "I should put this in a book."

"God, I hope not. That would be insane. I don't need any drama like that with Ty. Let's keep that in your romance books and out of my real life." I chuckle.

"I like him for both you and Kase," Allie says with conviction. "He loves you both, and he's good dad material for Kase. I've seen how patient he is with both of the boys.

Plus, I know Logan really likes him, too."

"Even Evan likes him," Beth playfully interjects.

Allie gets more serious. "He fits in with all of us. You lucked out with him, Mellie."

"I'll talk to him," I say to end this conversation. I'm really missing him right now. I've gotten so used to him being here with us and I never want what we have to end—whatever we're calling it. If this is as good as it ever gets for me, I'll take it.

I can't tell if there's really something here or I'm just naturally waiting for the other shoe to drop, because to be honest, it always has for me. I don't want that to happen with Ty, though.

Sensing a subject change, Beth and Allie slide the food closer and dig in.

"Are you excited for the farmers' market this weekend? Your first one ever! This is very exciting," Beth says.

"I am. Are you still available to help?"

"Of course. We're all hands on deck for you."

"And what about you, Allie? You ready to promote your new beautiful bakery?"

"I am so freaking nervous, but so excited." Allie exhales a big sigh.

"You're the most incredible baker, and people are so excited. Freedom Valley has needed this. The only other place to go to is the Freedom Bean, and they're always packed. This is needed, especially on Main Street," I assure her.

"Thank you." Allie smiles warmly.

"We've got this," Beth says.

"Yeah, we do."

And for once, I believe it. Things are going to be okay.

The door opens and Evan steps in. "Ladies," he says, greeting all of us. Then he walks over and wraps his arms around Beth, kissing her cheek.

"Hey, honey. I'm glad you're here."

"Me too. This looks good." He reaches over and takes some snacks from the board and pops them in his mouth.

"Thanks," Allie replies with a grin. She jumps as Beth kicks her under the table and gives her a look.

"What?" His eyes narrow. "What are you three scheming about? You are up to something." He scans the room, looking for clues.

Beth clears her throat. "So, you know how we have a bun in the oven?"

"Yeah," he says, looking at her sideways.

"Well, we baked you something. Can you go get it out of the kitchen?" Beth asks.

"Weird, but okay." He sighs as he strides into the back and we hear him open and shut one of the ovens before opening up another one.

"Which one?" he calls out.

"Bring them both," Allie calls back.

He comes out carrying the two buns Allie placed in there. He looks confused. "Why do you have two buns in your oven?"

"Why do you?" I ask with a smile.

His face falls in shock as he looks at Beth excitedly. "Do we?"

She nods, her eyes filling with tears. "Yes, there's two!"

He drops the buns to the floor and pulls her out of her chair into the biggest hug. He rests his forehead on hers. "There's two!" They both jump excitedly.

"Aww, you two, don't make them fall out," Allie says, wiping her eyes.

Just then, Logan comes in the front door and takes in all the commotion. "Why is there bread on the floor?"

"Those are Beth and Evan's buns from the oven."

Logan just sighs. "This family is so confusing." He picks up the buns and shakes his head as he walks over to Allie.

Allie laughs and pulls him into her arms. "We're having two nieces or nephews."

His eyes light up. "Oh, wow, congratulations, guys!" He claps Evan on the back and hugs Beth.

My heart is happy. I can't wait to tell Ty. And something about watching this happen for Beth and Evan makes me realize that I want this with Ty.

CHAPTER 20

~

Mellie

We have options.

Vibrant-colored spring flowers hang from the wrought-iron black lampposts on Main Street. I love the special charm of Freedom Valley's main drag. I've always enjoyed walking along and looking at the shops, seeing the local businesses that make Freedom Valley a popular small town to visit.

Preston's office has a brick exterior and a fresh black and gold sign out front with his name on it: Preston Steele, Attorney for Freedom Valley. I head in to find a receptionist desk piled high with papers and boxes. By the looks of it, I'm guessing he still hasn't hired an office manager.

I text him that I'm here whenever he's ready for me. His door quickly opens and he comes down the hall looking frazzled, running his hand through his hair. "Hey, Mellie, how's it going?"

"I'm good. Thanks for meeting with me."

"Come on back." He motions to follow him, and we step into his office, not bothering to shut the door because we're the only ones here. I sit across from him at his desk. He pulls out a folder with a picture of Bradley in his law enforcement uniform, and I wince just seeing him. A nervous buzz fills me, and I put my hand on my chest, my palms sweating nervously.

Preston clears his throat. "There's no new news."

"Okay..." I take a deep breath and prepare for this conversation.

"He does have a new girlfriend who's now living at your old house, and it looks like she's involved with drugs like he is, but we're still gathering intel on that." He gives me a minute to process, and when I don't say anything, he continues, "We have options, Mellie. This guy's a corrupt cop, and we can bury him with this information, make him fold and give you your divorce and sole custody. Or we can get him arrested and try to get him put away. It's up to you."

"Do I have to decide right now?" I stare at the folder on his desk, feeling overwhelmed. "Because I kind of like pretending he doesn't exist and not having to deal with him at the current moment."

"Nope, you don't have to decide right now. We have all the information we need. We can just sit tight for a while. I see no reason to make a move until you feel right about everything."

"Yeah." I sigh deeply, digesting this heavy information. "Thanks for doing this. I really appreciate it."

"Hey, it's no problem. I hear everyone in town talking about your farmers' market and how excited they are for it. Great job getting that all going, by the way."

"Thanks, I'm having fun with it all." I look around at his office in disarray. "You still haven't hired an office manager?"

"No, I've been swamped. But I'll find someone soon hopefully."

"I bet you will. Maybe put a sign up on the community board at Allie's bakery?"

He taps his pen toward me. "Now that's a good idea."

"Sometimes I have those," I tease as I stand. "I better get back to the inn, but thanks for everything. See you, Preston."

CHAPTER 21

Ty

One more thing...

I'm relieved my mom's going to be okay, but I'm still coming down from the big shock and scare she gave us this week with her heart. She's been overweight and struggling with her health for a long time. She's agreed to make some health changes, and her heart stuff is stabilized for now with medication. I'm worried about her, but I'm hopeful she's going to start doing better. She's a fighter, and she's determined to get healthy.

I don't like being away as much as I have this past year,

and it sucks not being able to get home as much as I'd like to see my parents. What will I do when the job wraps up? Being here in Alabama has made me realize that this doesn't feel like home anymore. Home feels like it's back in Freedom Valley, with Mellie and Kase. After I'm done with this assignment, I'm hoping to come back home more often and have my parents come see us, too.

I bring my mom flowers and a card to the hospital. I take a seat beside her bed in the chair that we've all taken turns sleeping in on and off for the past few days.

"Momma, I love you. I'm so glad you're okay."

"Thank you, honey. I'm just ready to get this surgery over with. Take care of your body and don't do like I did."

"You're going to be just fine."

"I want to be strong and healthy and live a long life so I can be a grandma for your babies," she says, looking hopefully at me.

I sigh, taking her hand in mine. She has been after me for years to make her a grandma. She and my dad have always wanted me to settle down. I never tell her anything about my assignments, but I do want to tell her about Mellie and Kase.

"I did meet someone, actually. I love her."

Her face softens. "Tell me about her. I need a good distraction."

"I can't say much just yet, but she has a little boy. He's four."

Her eyes light up. "A little boy?"

"Yeah. Nova's with them right now. Keeping an eye on them for me."

"Oh, I miss my Nova girl."

"This assignment will be wrapping up soon. It's been a long one. I'm at a point where I have to decide whether I'm going to take on a new commitment or get out."

"What do you want to do?"

"I want to settle down. I want a wife and a family. I don't think I can have that with the ATF."

"What's stopping you? There are a lot of jobs out there. You can come back and work with Dad anytime. He wants to retire and leave the shop to you."

"I know, but I like it up there. I don't like that it's so far from you guys, though. I want you to be near me when I have a family."

"We're not married to Alabama. I'm fixing to retire next year, and your daddy has talked about selling the business if you aren't interested in it. We can go wherever. I just have to know where that is."

"I can't tell you that yet, but I know you'd like it there. It's real pretty, and the people are real nice."

"I think it'll all come together. When it's right, it'll be right, and you'll just *know*. We'll work it all out."

"I need you to get healthy so you can come to my wedding someday and hold my babies." I take her hand in mine, feeling scared. I can't imagine not having her here.

"I'm going to do everything I can, I promise."

And that's why I'm driving to Mellie's hometown to do a little recon. I want to see for myself what I'm dealing with so that I can know more about how to keep them safe. After leaving my parents, I drive two hours to Diamond, the small Mississippi town where she's from. I think about what life must have been like for them and how much they've been through. It pisses me off, but I need to focus on gathering information so I know what we're dealing with here.

A couple of quick Google searches bring up her old address. It's hard to imagine they had a whole other life here before they came to Freedom Valley. I set out on a jog not far from the house so that I can "run" by. As I turn the corner, I see the black semi-truck minus the trailer parked at the end of the street that I'm assuming is Mitch's.

I'm debating it, but my gut says it's a good move to try to talk to him. Evan gave me the information that I needed if I did see Mitch. He knew Mitch wouldn't talk to me unless I could let him know I was legit. I jog by and see him out working on his pick-up out front. I stop jogging and approach him.

Mitch is a big guy, the type who could probably be

intimidating to some, but he's a good guy in my book. Knowing he helped Mellie and Kase when he didn't have to, putting himself in jeopardy... He just did it because it was the right thing to do, simple as that.

"You Mitch?"

Mitch looks up from under the hood of his car. He eyes me warily. "Who wants to know?"

"Hey, man, I'm Ty." I talk to him like we're old friends in case her ex is watching from across the street.

He stands and wipes his hands on a rag from his back pocket, eyeing me.

"I'm a friend of a friend of yours, from up north. Checking in on the status of things around here," I say, keeping eye contact with him.

"Don't know you or what you're talking about," he says as he goes back to working on his truck.

"Our mutual friend told me to say, 'Remember the time Halo ate your hat and shit on your bed?'"

Mitch breaks into laughter and turns around to face me again, this time his face relaxed. "I had to sleep on the floor for a week it stunk so bad. Halo was a bastard. I hated that old K9."

Now that he knows I'm legit with that connecting piece of information to Evan, I feel like he might open up.

"Anyway, just out for a jog," I say casually as I survey his tools out of habit. "Passing through. Checking in."

"How are they?" he asks quietly, sliding a wrench out of his tool bag and leaning over the hood again.

"Good. Real good. Any updates from around here?"

"It's quiet. He's got a new lady now," he says, not looking up from the truck as he speaks.

"You think he's still looking for them?"

"Oh, I *know* he's still looking. I think Mellie's a loose end for him that he wants to tie up. Word on the street is he doesn't want her found; he wants her dead." He now looks at me with worried eyes.

My stomach drops and my fists clench for a minute. "That'll never happen."

"When you see her, tell her something for me?"

"Sure." Again, out of habit, I lean over and connect a wire to his alternator and hand him the socket to tighten it.

He looks at the wire and back at me curiously. "I'll be damned. Been trying to figure this out for an hour."

"It's no problem. Raised by a mechanic." I shrug. "What can I tell her for you?"

"Remind her what I said about starting over." He looks at me thoughtfully.

"I can do that."

Suddenly, the garage door across the street opens and a truck backs out. I turn my body to face Mitch, but I keep the truck in my peripheral vision so I can get a visual on the driver.

A bark sounds at the side of the fence, and I look over to see a small, dark brown Dachshund. The truck pulls back and I'm thankful I have a hat and sunglasses on as I see her ex driving the truck. He glares at Mitch and drives by. He rolls through the stop sign at the end of the street and speeds off. Nice.

"That him?"

"Yup."

Jesus. Being here in person and seeing him for myself makes me feel a whole lot closer to all of this.

"Is that Sassy?" I ask, not moving my head toward the house in case we're being watched by the new girlfriend.

"Yep. I've been wanting to get the dog out of there, too," he says, not looking over there either and instead looking at his truck, no doubt that we're probably being watched. "Just haven't figured out how to do that."

This gives me an idea, although I don't dare say anything out loud.

"It was nice to meet you, Mitch. You have a good day!" I call as I break off into a jog again, pushing my sunglasses up on my face.

He waves and continues to work on his truck. I take the long way back to my rental car and add in a few extra alleys to make sure I'm not followed.

I won't underestimate Bradley. He's a cop, after all. An asshole and a piece of shit, but that doesn't mean he can't be smart. Most people make the mistake of underestimating people, but I never put people in boxes. I just evaluate and cover my tracks. Always. And that's what makes me a good agent. No slip-ups.

Going to Mitch's was probably not the best idea, but I had to know. And now I do. Now there's just one more thing I need to do before I leave...

CHAPTER 22

⌒

Mellie

He completes us.

My very first farmers' market is today, and I was so excited that I set my alarm for four a.m., wanting to be up extra early to get everything ready. I get up and check in on Kase, who's spooning Nova, her back curled into his belly, his little arm draped over her. She looks up briefly as I peek in. When she sees it's just me, her head drops back down again.

I miss Ty, and I'm ready for him to come home. Having him gone has made me realize I don't want to live in the bunkhouse without him. I want him home. *Home.* This place has become home. Not just Freedom Valley and the inn, but the bunkhouse with Ty. I was happy over at the inn and in our little loft, and honestly, I thought that could be enough for us. But then we met Ty, and everything got even better, which I couldn't have imagined.

Nova's even bonded with us and become a part of our family, too. I can't imagine not having either of them in our lives now.

I didn't think it would be possible to find a love like this. I didn't love Bradley after I realized who he really was, I didn't even like him. I loved what he should have been but what he never could be because he was so evil.

But Ty? I'm hopelessly in love with him. I've fallen off the deep end in love. And it's both scary and exciting at the same time. I love the way he is with Kase. I love his heart. He's easy to be with and he feels safe. He makes me happy. Truly happy. And I haven't felt that way in a very long time.

I brew coffee and tidy up the kitchen before I head over to the pole barn and load up Ty's truck with the baskets of produce I packaged up late last night, pleased with how all the details are coming together.

I wake Kase and get him ready for the day, and he's so excited to be my helper. He feeds Nova and refills her water while I get ready. I put on my Support Local Farmers T-shirt and my favorite beaded earrings that a local artisan made and will be selling today. I love seeing the community come together like this to share their treasures that they either grew or made.

I load Nova and Kase up in the truck and drive over to the inn for breakfast. I have the day off from cleaning, so it feels nice to be able to have a visit with everyone and just relax.

Sasha greets us with a smile and a plate of breakfast casserole and fresh fruit.

Kase and I sit with Nova under his chair, always on guard, and enjoy our breakfast visiting with Evan and Beth.

Margie comes in behind them. "Good morning. How's my boy?" She squeezes Kase's shoulders and kisses his head.

"I'm good. Did you know that Momma said I can pick out three things from the market? Three," he says, holding up three fingers.

"Oh, yeah, what are you choosing?" She takes a seat next to him and Sasha hands her a plate. "Thank you, Sash."

"I don't know yet. But cookies if there's cookies." He scoops a bite of casserole into his mouth.

"Does she know yet?" I whisper to Beth.

She shakes her head and nudges Evan under the table.

He clears his throat. "Beth and I need your help picking out names," he tells his mom.

"I thought you had a name picked out."

"We do. We need another one."

"Why do you need another..." She covers her mouth with her hand. "Oh." She starts to cry. "Are there two?" she asks through happy tears.

Evan confirms proudly. "There are two."

"Oh, honey." She walks over and gathers them both in a hug.

Sasha smiles. "I'm so happy for you both. Lots of new life at the inn."

As we finish enjoying our breakfast, Sasha asks me, "Are you ready for today?"

"I'm so ready. How about you? Are you excited for your seasoning blends to flavor every kitchen in Freedom Valley?" I say to Sasha.

"I am. Wouldn't have them if your herbs hadn't helped me make them all. So, thanks for that." She gets up to clear some plates. "I set up a salad bar for an easy lunch for the guests today. I'm excited to get out there and see how my little business can do."

"What blends did you decide on?"

"My maple bourbon, fried chicken, and barbeque seasonings. Those are my top three that people request."

"Those are the best," Evan agrees.

"Well, let's head out and get set up. First annual farmers' market in the books," I say eagerly. "This is history in the making for the inn."

As we head out, Evan pats me on the back. "Great job, Mellie. You did so good with all this."

I'm happy knowing I contributed something here. I like working at the inn and being around all these people who have become like family to me, but I love growing food and feeding lots of people things that I grew from a seed. It's like new life in a new place, something that is very close to my heart. These people accepted me into their community and gave me space to grow. It's only fitting that I do the same to give back.

"Thanks," I say. Nova jumps up into the truck next to Kase in the back. "You ready, guys?" I ask them.

Nova's tongue hangs out the side of her mouth as usual and she takes a moment to slurp Kase's cheek with an affectionate kiss. He giggles and says, "Ready."

We head to the back lot to set up at our table where Evan and Logan help me unload everything. Beth helps with my signs, I put on my gardening apron, and then we're in business.   People begin to start trickling in. I see tables of fresh flowers, herbs, baked goods, plants, pottery, handmade crafts, early spring vegetables, and more.

Kase asks if he and Caleb can go with Beth to walk around, and I nod. "Have fun," I call after them.

The farmers' market is off to a great start, my vegetables and herbs halfway gone by the time I feel arms wrap around me, and I breathe in his familiar scent, the smell of home. I close my eyes and smile as I turn, wrapping my arms around him. "Ty," I breathe.

"Miss me?"

"So much." I smile, taking him in. I'm trying to play it

cool, but I have zero chill in me right now. I'm grinning stupidly and I can't stop looking at him. I stand on my tip toes and kiss him, pulling him closer.

"I missed you, too." He stops and looks around. "Where's Kase?"

I reach for his hand. "He's shopping with Caleb and Beth."

"This all turned out great," he says, pulling up my hand and kissing the back of it, taking in the farmers' market that is still in full swing, buzzing with activity.

"Thank you." I smile as I turn to help a customer and bag up their produce for them.

"They'll be so happy to see you." I wrap my arms around him again. As much as I want this farmers' market to happen, I'll be glad when we can be alone and catch up on everything. "How's your mom? I want to hear all about your trip."

"On the mend." He steps aside so I can help a customer with some fresh herbs and after she chooses, he helps her bag them up.

"I told her about you and Kase," he tells me after the next customer leaves. He told his mom about me. My heart swells and my eyes widen as he says, "That I found a girl and a little boy that I'm in love with."

"Oh, yeah?"

"What are we doing tonight?"

"I was going to keep it simple after a long day."

"I can grill up some burgers for us."

"I'll make dessert," I say.

"Babe." He tips his head at me, calling me out. "You will commandeer dessert from Allie or Sasha. That is not the same as making dessert."

"What can I say?" I shrug and grin. "I am what I am."

He laughs. "I missed this with you." He pulls me in and kisses my cheek. "Get something good."

"I always do."

Just then, Nova runs up, excited to see Ty. She jumps up and tries to kiss him. He leans down and pets her, kisses her head, and hugs her close. "Hey, girl. I missed you, too. I didn't know that you brought her."

"Of course we did." I smile as I wave to one of the customers who walks by.

He turns his head and looks for Kase, holding his arms out as Kase runs to him and hugs him, his little arms around Ty's sides. "Ty! You came back!"

"Of course I did. I missed you."

"Nova just stole two peanut butter cookies from Allie. She got in big trouble. Big," he says, holding his hands out wide.

"Aww, Nova, what did you do?" he asks her, scolding her but still smiling.

I know Kase is watching to see how Ty reacts to Nova getting into trouble, his little hand resting on her protectively. He looks relieved when he sees Ty's reaction, and this makes me feel both sad and encouraged. Ultimately,

I'm so relieved that we're done with Bradley's abuse, and I'm hopeful that Kase will see that not all men hurt people, that Ty is safe for us.

Ty pulls both Kase and Nova in for a big hug. "I'm going to grill some burgers up for you tonight, bud. You want to help me?"

Kase visibly relaxes and his little arm wraps around Ty as he nods.

Just then, Logan and Evan walk up and clap Ty on the back to have a bro moment. I see them all standing around, hands stuffed in pockets, laughing and talking while Kase curls up on a blanket behind my booth watching something on my phone with Nova tucked into him.

Yes. This will do quite nicely. I love my life here. He completes us in ways I never thought possible.

CHAPTER 23

Mellie

I like us.

Ty and I have both been busy during the past week since he's been home, but when we're home at the same time, I treasure our time together. The garden has really taken off and every spare moment that I have, I'm out there with Kase weeding, watering, and harvesting. I get my work at the inn done quickly and head out to the gardens to work and play. Because that's what it feels like to me: play.

We have a picnic table set up by the greenhouse and we have been packing a dinner to go so we can eat it out here before Ty goes to work in the evenings. I love our new life and our new routine. At the end of the days, we're dirty, tired, and happy.

I'm bundling up produce for Sasha when I see Ty coming down the garden path. I stand and wipe my hands on the back of my pants. "Hey, you. How'd you sleep?"

"Not as good as I would if you'd been beside me." He steals a quick kiss.

"I'm all sweaty and dirty." I laugh and pull back.

"I don't care. Where's Kase?" he asks, looking around.

"He's over there playing with his trucks." I point to the edge of the gardens.

"Are you ready to eat? I brought dinner," he says as he waves at Kase.

"Ty!" Kase calls, running his little legs in his boots, struggling to get through the dirt with Nova following closely behind him.

"Yes, so hungry. It's been a long day."

He grabs Kase and swings him up on top of his shoulders and turns his hat around front-facing. "It's looking good out here, Mel. What are these?" he asks, pointing to rows I'm adding more dirt on top of.

"Potatoes. I have to add more dirt and then just let them keep growing."

"That's incredible. Let's eat, and then you can give me an updated tour. Things are really taking off so fast."

We walk hand in hand to the picnic table with Kase on

Ty's shoulders, and if you looked at this from the outside, you might see a normal happy family. Even if this is new, I want this. I look up at him and he smiles back down at me.

"What are you thinking?" he asks.

"I like this. I like us."

"Yeah, me too," he says as he swings Kase off of his shoulders and onto the picnic table, ruffling his hair. "Being good for your mom, Kase?"

"Yeah," he says as I help Kase clean his hands off with wipes and sanitizer.

"What do you need help with out here?" he asks me.

"Nothing, just your company," I say as I slide onto the picnic table and motion for him to join me. He slides in next to me and sets out our sandwiches and salads.

My face feels warm and I smile, taking a bite of my salad. It feels good to have a man encourage me and help me. A night and day change from our old life. I look over at Kase happily eating and swinging his feet. His life is so much better now, and that's what matters to me. He deserves this. I deserve this. And this moment is when I decide I won't let anyone or anything take this life away from us. If Bradley wants to come for us, he better be ready for a war.

We wrap up dinner and walk through the gardens hand in hand. Ty pulls me in and kisses me, holding me tight to him.

"I don't want to work tonight," he admits, his hand wrapping under my bottom as he pulls me in possessively.

"We'll be around in the morning and have breakfast ready for you if you want. Several of the hens have started laying and we have a few farm-fresh eggs," I offer.

"I'd like that. Alright, I have to head out. See you in the morning." He kisses me, my arms wrapping around his neck and kissing him back, not wanting to stop. I pull back and look at him, and he says, "We need a date night. Can you get a sitter for Kase so we can go out, just us? I want some time with you." His eyes smolder.

"Yes." I'm still breathless from the kiss. "That sounds good. Maybe he can do a sleepover one night with Caleb."

"Even better," he says, and I know what he's thinking by the way he's already eye-fucking me.

"Come here, Kase, Nova!" he calls out to them. I love how he says goodbye and gives Kase a hug every time he leaves. Watching Kase get more and more comfortable with Ty is worth it. And maybe Allie was onto something: maybe Ty needs us just as much as we need him.

The next day, I bring Sasha a few overflowing baskets of produce. Guests are raving about the delicious meals she's been making with it. Her meals are already a major hit, but now that she has farm-fresh produce and is starting to get more eggs in, it's really kicking up a notch. Pete added seven more chickens, and watching the coop come together has been great.

The community garden is a smashing success, and we have volunteers working daily to keep it going, along with the main inn garden and our lavender garden that I keep up with. Every time I come through and smell everything, it feels instantly calming. This is a peaceful place that leaves me feeling grateful every single day. I fall into bed every night feeling fulfilled and exhausted, but in the best possible way.

I go to Allie's bakery to grab a cup of coffee and check in with everyone. It's busy and bustling with customers sitting on laptops, people having coffee, and chatting. It smells like fresh coffee and buttery baked goods. Two of my favorite things. My top favorite place is my garden, but this is becoming a close second. Allie waves me over as I walk in.

"Hey, Mellie. What can I get you?" She smiles proudly behind the counter.

"Just a coffee with cream," I say, pulling out my wallet.

"Your money is no good here." She laughs as she puts a lid on a coffee and slides it over to me. "Come hang with me a minute. We just hit a lull, and I need a break." We sit side by side on a navy-blue, velvet couch. "So, I have a funny prank I want to pull on the guys for Beth's gender reveal dinner at the inn on Saturday," she tells me.

"What are you thinking?"

"I bought all of these plaid shirts on clearance that all

match, and we have to convince the guys to wear them so they'll all show up wearing the same shirt, not knowing."

I snort. "Okay, let's do it."

She walks over and reaches behind the counter. She pulls out a cream and beige plaid shirt and tosses it to me. "Here's Ty's."

"We're so bad." I shake my head. But deep down, I love being considered as a couple with Ty. "So, what else is new?" I ask Allie, sipping my coffee.

"Just living my dream. The bakery is amazing, Logan is traveling a bit this week for work. He gets back home Friday night in time for the gender reveal."

"I can't wait to find out. What do you think they're having?"

"Well, I already know, because I'm making the gender reveal cakes." She covers her big grin with her hand.

"I'm so excited." I check my watch. "I gotta head back."

"See you Saturday!"

"See you," I shout, laughing at the thought of them all showing up at the same time and realizing they're all twinning.

CHAPTER 24

~

Ty

So, make me one.

"Why am I wearing this shirt again?" I ask Mellie, confused.

"It's a gift. Don't you like it?" Mellie says, her eyes not meeting mine.

"Yep, it's nice, I just didn't expect you to get me a shirt. Is it a special occasion?"

"We better go so we won't be late," Mellie says as she rushes to grab her purse.

"I'll make us late," I whisper as I pull her in toward me, cupping her bottom and holding her tight. She melts into me as she leans up to kiss me, wrapping her arms around my neck.

The problem is that kissing is all we've been doing, but I just feel like I need this job to wrap up so I can be honest with her before we go any further. I feel like it's even more of a betrayal if we go there and she doesn't know. It feels like I'm living a lie, so I need her to know first. It just feels wrong otherwise.

Kase's footsteps come down the hall and she pulls back, looking like she'd rather stay home, too. "Okay, we really have to go."

We've fallen into easy days together that just feel right. We do things as a family, and everything has fallen into a good place.

When we get to the inn, I carry in the plate of cheese and crackers we put together. Evan opens the door with an expression that looks less than pleased.

"Oh, you too? Beth!" Evan yells, but he's shaking his head and smiling. I see Pete is also wearing the same plaid shirt that Evan and I have on.

Okay, now I get it. They've pranked us.

"Just wait until Logan gets here," Beth snickers.

I look over at Mellie and shake my head, trying to hold back a smirk. Sasha is laughing and so is Beth, who is cackling so hard she looks like she's crying. Pete looks up and rolls his eyes as he takes the platter from me and opens it and digs in. I follow him over to where the appetizers are to hide from all the mockery.

Just then, Logan and Allie come in. "Hey everyone," she calls.

Logan follows behind her carrying the cake and he stops in the doorway and deadpans, "Really?" as he takes in all of us wearing the same shirt. "Whose idea was this?"

Allie, Beth, and Mellie can't keep it together. Logan, Evan, Pete, and I cross our arms, all in our matching plaid shirts, and shake our heads, an action that seems to make them laugh even harder. Mellie pulls out her phone and makes us all pose for a picture.

"Oh, this will be great for photos later," Margie says as she clasps her hands together, thrilled. "All of my boys, matching."

The shirt prank I honestly didn't mind, but hearing Margie include me with everyone and us fitting in here as a family feels good. Feels right. This is what I wanted. The everyday life with someone I love.

I meet Mellie's gaze and she melts a little. "You mad at the shirts?"

"No, I'm not mad. I just... I love this. I love us."

"I love us, too," she says.

"I want to talk to you about something later." I'm starting to feel guilty, like I need to tell her about the ATF. I'm torn because it's an active assignment—one I'm not supposed to tell anyone about—but she deserves to know.

"Mellie, can you help me?" Sasha calls from the dining room.

"I'll be right back," she says, laying her hand on my shoulder and heading down the hall.

"You two are so sweet," Allie calls from across the counter. "You're next!"

"Next for what?" I ask.

"For a family," she scoffs.

"I hope so," I confirm.

Her smile widens, pleased to hear this. "Well, I'll be. You really do love her."

"Them. I love them," I correct her with a smile.

"I'm so happy for you," she says, coming around and giving me a hug.

"Thanks," I say as I reach for Kase and pull him toward me and flip him in my arms, a move he loves. His giggles are contagious, and I can't help but smile when he does that.

Evan nods at us, and there it is: the Harper approval. He nods for me to follow him, and we head down toward his office.

"Did you see Mitch?" he asks.

"Seems like a great guy."

"He is."

"The ex drove by, but I didn't make contact."

"Did you tell her that you went there?"

"Not yet. I'm waiting to wrap up my job at Larkin, and I

need to talk to her about some things." I sigh.

Evan reads me and says, "Don't wait too long. Not sure how that's going to go."

Hearing this makes me nervous and confirms I need to talk to her. Soon. I'm just not sure how to go about it.

"Alright, guys! Cake first! Then we can eat real food and discuss the babies," Allie calls out.

Mellie and Margie come in and finish setting up a few things, and then Mellie settles in next to me.

Beth and Evan are at the front table and put their arms around each other. "Okay, are you ready to find out what baby A and baby B are?" Beth asks. "Any guesses?"

"Yes!" the room chatters as everyone throws out their guesses.

Evan and Beth hold the knife together and cut into the first cake and the piece slides out: blue.

"Boy!" Evan booms happily as he pulls Beth in for a kiss.

"One down and one to go!" Logan calls out, recording this with his phone.

"Okay, and baby B is..." Beth says as they cut into the next cake.

"Girl!" They call out as they slide out a pink piece of cake.

Evan pulls Beth in for a hug, and they look at each other

excitedly. "One of each," he says as his eyes are still locked on Beth.

I reach for Mellie and pull her toward me. She leans into my chest, tucking under my chin. I wrap my arms around her and squeeze her to me.

Mellie looks up at me like she's trying to gauge what I'm thinking, and she says softly, "You're going to make a great dad someday."

I kiss her neck and whisper in her ear, "So make me one."

Her relieved sigh was all I needed to know that she wants that, too.

She wants to be with me. This reaffirms that I'm making the right decision, and that decision is going to be taking place real soon.

CHAPTER 25

Mellie

You're free.

It's hot today and I'm covered in dirt. Kase is with Caleb while I harvest for the next farmers' market. My AirPods are in my ears so I'm not aware of anyone approaching me until I feel someone tap my shoulder. My head whips around and I jump back with my shovel in hand, breathing heavily.

It's just Preston, looking as terrified as I feel. "You scared me." I hold my hand to my chest. "What are you doing here?"

He looks forlorn. "I had to come talk to you and tell you something in person. I texted Ty, he's on his way, too. He'll be here any minute."

"Where's Kase?" I frantically set the shovel down and reach for my phone, assuming something is wrong with him.

"He's fine. He's with Margie at the inn."

"What's going on?" I demand, swallowing and shaking my head. He's found us. If he's here... Ty comes jogging down the field toward us and I look from him to Preston. "Is Bradley here? Are we in danger?"

"No, he's not here." Preston nods at Ty, who puts his arm around me.

"What happened?" Ty asks.

Preston looks like he's not sure where to begin, but finally speaks, "I found out from our investigator that Bradley is now deceased." He looks pointedly at me. "It's over, Mellie."

I feel like the earth is spinning and I sink down to the dirt, Ty sits next to me, still holding me, and Preston kneels beside me. My heart is racing and so many emotions are flooding me. Grief, relief, anger, confusion. I don't even know what to say, what to think about this. How to process what he's telling me right now.

"What ha—what happened?"

"He was killed in what looks like a drug deal gone wrong. It appears the girlfriend was killed, too. I wanted to tell you in person. I know this is upsetting information to take in."

I nod, not even sure what to say. "But it's over?" I whisper.

"It's over, Mellie. He's gone."

Ty's arms pull me in close but he says nothing. He's just

with me.

I'm filled with sadness for what Bradley has missed out on, anger for what he's done, and relief for us to finally not have to live in hiding anymore. Ultimately, it's the feeling of relief that stays with me, and for the first time in a long time, I feel a sense of peace.

"This feels... weird. I don't know what to feel. What do I tell Kase?" I look back and forth between them in shock. They just stay with me while I try to process everything. "I'm safe here now. I can be me."

"It's overwhelming, and it's going to take some time to feel everything," Preston says. He nods at Ty. "You got her?"

"Yeah, I got her." Ty pulls me closer.

"Thank you for coming here. For telling me in person. I really appreciate that." I look at Preston and tears fill my eyes. This isn't the worst day of my life, but it's a mile marker.

Ty pushes open the gate to the lavender garden and we walk inside, his arm around me.

"I thought I'd feel differently if this happened, but I just feel sad."

"Grief is weird." Ty holds my hand firmly. "There's really no handbook. Everyone grieves differently. Sometimes people are angry, hurt, or sad, or all of the above, especially when it's for someone who abused you."

"I'm relieved, but I also feel sad that two people died. And one being someone I shared a child with. I don't know what to tell Kase." I can't believe I'm feeling bad for Bradley even after what he's done, but I am.

"I'm supposed to go into work, but I can call in," Ty tells me.

"I think I need to be alone for a while. I'm okay, I just need to think about everything. I think I'll work some more out here and then see you in the morning, okay?"

"Mellie…" I hear over my shoulder and look to Beth and Allie coming toward us.

"You sure?" Ty asks, still holding onto my hand. I can tell he doesn't want to leave me.

"I'll be alright. Thank you for coming. I love you."

He kisses the top of my head and says, "Love you. Text me if you need me and I'll come right back. Okay?"

"I will."

"What happened? Preston just left looking worried and wouldn't tell us anything. He said we had to ask you."

"My ex-husband died."

Allie looks shocked. "Holy shit. I was only kidding about throwing him off a cliff, I swear."

"Wow. What happened?" Beth asks.

"It's over." I shrug. "He can't hurt us anymore, and I no longer have to hide from him."

"You're free. But I can also see where there's sadness, too," Beth says, her eyes searching mine. I know she knows grief having lost her husband and baby to a drunk driving accident.

"There is. I'm sad that he couldn't be the husband and father he should have been, but he did terrible things. He was a terrible person."

"I'm sorry, Mellie. You built this life here and you did it while carrying all of this weight, but now you can build your life with Ty and finally be happy. That doesn't mean you can't still grieve your old life, though."

"Yeah, you're right." I wipe my face and lean against Beth as she pulls me into a hug.

"It's going to be okay. You have us. You're safe. Kase is safe. We've all got you," Beth says.

Allie reaches in and pulls me in for a hug on the other side. "What's going to happen now?"

"I guess I can just live my life now and finally stop looking over my shoulder. It's a blessing in so many ways." I blow out a deep breath.

"Whatever you feel, just feel it. You didn't deserve the hell you went through."

I nod and wipe my eyes.

"But don't forget you do deserve the new life you have here. You have to believe that. Every good thing that comes your way, you deserve."

"I love you guys," I say, pulling them in for a hug.

"We love you, too," Allie says. "It takes a village and we're each other's."

"It smells really good out here," Beth says.

"It's a lavender garden. It's supposed to be calming." I smile and blink back tears. Tears of relief and tears of confusion. Ty was right, grief is weird.

"Come on," Allie says. "Let us help you wrap up your day. What can we do?"

"Just being here with me is nice," I admit. "Thanks for coming out here."

"Of course," Allie says.

"We love you, Mellie," Beth adds.

CHAPTER 26

Mellie

But what if I never really had him?

It's taken me a few days to recover from the shock of everything, and I'm still working through my feelings. If someone would have told me a year ago that this is where I'd be, I don't think I would have ever believed it, but I feel like things are going to be okay.

I finish another audiobook and tuck my AirPods into their case. I've binge listened to a whole series this week that was funny and made me laugh out loud, and I'm glad that listening to romance books has gotten easier for me. I used to get sad listening to all of these happily ever afters, but now? I think they might be a possibility for me, too, and that gives me hope.

Thanks to Beth's current state of nesting, she kept up with all of my laundry today. The last load is in the dryer, and she has shooed me away for the rest of the day.

Evan puts away some tools in the bottom of the shed as I wrap up my cleaning for the day. He turns and says, "You know you can move back if you want." He must pick up on my hesitation because he says, "I'm glad things are going good at the bunkhouse with Ty."

I bite my lip, not sure what to say. "It's going well, we like it out there. Kase has gotten pretty attached to Nova," I say, turning to stack soap on the carts, trying to hide my smile.

"Oh, just Nova? Not attached to Ty?" Evan laughs.

"We like Ty, too."

"Uh-huh. I've seen you guys, Mel. He seems to make you happy."

I take this chance to catch up with Sasha for a minute while Kase colors with Caleb.

"Want to take Ty some dinner?" She stirs something that smells amazing over on the stovetop. Even Sasha loves having Ty around and often sends over meals for when he's working and can't make it to the inn.

"Sasha, I didn't know it could be like this. You were right...
I did find someone for me. And now that my ex is gone, I
have freedom to finally live my life."

She nods and looks over to me. It feels good to finally
explain everything to everyone here at the inn. I don't think
they were very surprised, and they probably knew something
had happened, but the best part is that they just love me for
who I am and not who I was. A broken single mom on the
run.

"Isn't Ty supposed to be waking up soon? Why don't you
take dinner to-go and eat with him, and I'll keep Kase with
me. You boys can help me make some mini pies," she tells
them.

"Yes! Chocolate," Caleb says as he drops his crayon and
raises his hands in excitement.

"Don't eat all the chocolate this time," Kase whispers.

"That's the best part," Caleb whispers back.

"Yeah, I can do that. I'll grab more produce for you, too, if
you need more," I tell her.

"Oh, yes, please. And that reminds me," she says, wiping
her hands on her towel. "Can you bring me back some basil,
oregano, and thyme, too?"

"Sure can." I smile with satisfaction.

"Thanks," she says as she bags up the to-go containers
for me.

I reach out to hug her. "Thanks, I'll be back in a bit."

"Take your time," she says, winking at the boys. "We have things to do, dough to eat."

This is my favorite time of year, and I love taking drives or walks and just looking at all of the plants and flowers blossoming all throughout the property. Can it get any better than this? Summer feels like it's flying by, and I don't want to miss out on a minute of it. This is my favorite season, where everything grows and thrives.

I pull up to the bunkhouse and head in, eager to see Ty. I catch myself humming to myself. This version of Mellie is a much better one than before. Preston had asked if we wanted to go back to our old names, but I said no. We got a fresh start, and this is who we are and where we live now. I love the life we've made here. Oh, and now I can finally get my New Hampshire driver's license.

Ty's truck and bike are out front, so I figure he must still be sleeping or getting ready. I step into the quiet house and find it just the way I left it this morning: tidy, with the dish towel draped over the front of the sink.

It sounds like he's on the phone, so I wait for him to come out of his room. I set out our food so he can eat right away before he has to leave for work. As he speaks, there's something about his voice that's different. His tone is commanding and professional, and I wonder who he's talking to. He's definitely not as relaxed as when he talks to Sam or Evan.

His footsteps sound from down the hall. He freezes in the doorway when he sees me.

The container I'm holding falls to the table and spills.

No. Just no. What I'm seeing right now can't be right. Are you fucking kidding me?

Ty is wearing navy tactical pants and a navy T-shirt with a flack vest that has ATF on the front, a gold badge next to it.

He's still on the phone. His eyes lock on mine and he says, "I'll call you right back." He hangs up the phone and stares at me, his eyes are full of fear and he looks pained. "Mellie." He looks miserable. "I couldn't tell you..." He starts to come toward me.

"Just stop." I hold up my hand. "I knew this thing between us was too good to be true. I knew it."

He takes a step toward me again, his face in agony. "I couldn't risk a two-year operation where lives are at stake. I couldn't. I'm so sorry."

"Nope." I'm oddly calm. I realize this is anger. Betrayal. "Don't." I just stare at him, wondering where I missed the signs, but then they flash through me and I realize they were there all along.

Toad not thinking he worked at Larkin.

Beth joking that he might be a secret agent.

It all starts clicking into place.

"Mellie, just listen," he begs. "Please. I can explain everything."

I just continue to stare at him, processing this. He was never going to stay here. He was here for work, and I don't even really know him. This was all lies.

"I don't even know you," I say finally.

"You do," he pleads. "I love you, Mellie."

"No. You're not who you said you were. You lied to me."

"I had to. I promise I'll tell you everything. I'm so sorry."

"You said you would be loyal to me. The most disloyal thing you did was get me to trust you when all along it was a lie."

"I am loyal, I promise. Mellie, please let me explain." He's begging now. Pleading. His eyes have tears in them and his voice cracks.

I shake my head. No. This is it. I'm done. I won't be lied to again, not by another man. I don't need this. I never needed this. I made a mistake again. With a man in law enforcement, at that.

He puts his face in his hands and looks up at me, his eyes red and his face stricken. "If I could have told you, I would have. I wanted to tell you. So many times, I almost did. It was so hard for me. You have no idea."

"Hard for you? How hard is it for you? You let me live a lie here with you. I thought we had something together. You even said you loved me," I shriek at this point, starting to shake.

"I do love you. I love you so much. Please let me explain."

"Is that why you wouldn't sleep with me? Because this was all fake?"

"No, it's not fake, I promise. I just wanted you to really know before—"

"Just go," I cut him off as I move behind the kitchen island and cross my arms, looking out the window. "Just go!" I scream at him.

"I love you so much. I'll be back tonight. Please let me explain..."

I shake my head and refuse to look at him.

He walks back down the hall and comes back carrying a big navy duffle bag. "I promise I'll explain everything when I get back. I love you, Mellie." He doesn't come to me, but finally turns and leaves, the big ATF logo on the back of his vest giving me chills. I slide to the floor and watch him out the slider door as he slides into his truck and leaves.

How many times did Bradley hurt us and then pull on that uniform and head to work like nothing had happened?

Ty knew my ex was a police officer, and he knew I was upset about how the local police covered for him whenever he abused me. He had so many opportunities to tell me the truth, to be honest. I wouldn't have told anyone. I let him in, yet he couldn't do the same.

Tears stream down my face as I go to the greenhouse and sink into the grass. I hide my face in my hands and cry. I've never been much of a crier, but I need this. Tears I've pushed down for the past year spill out, and I cry for so long and so hard I don't think I'll ever be able to stop.

I must have fallen asleep in the grass by the lavender field and don't wake up until dark when I feel arms around me, shaking me gently. *Ty.* Then I remember what he did, and he's gone. It's Evan, and he's worried.

"Are you okay, Mel?"

"It's Ty."

He searches my face. "What happened?"

"Did you know he's ATF?" I whisper.

He just nods. "I kinda knew, Mel. I couldn't say anything, but we had talked about some things before he went home, so I had a good idea."

"I went to the cabin to take him dinner and he came out in his uniform, getting ready to leave."

"What'd he say?"

"He said he loved me, but he couldn't tell me."

"Hey, it's okay." He pulls me into a hug.

"Can I please move back to the garden shed?"

"Yes, you can always come back. But are you sure that's really what you want to do?"

"He could have told me."

His head tilts down. "Sometimes it's not that easy."

"Everything I know about him is a lie."

After a while, Evan finally says, "I don't think that could be true with the way he loves you guys but come back to the garden shed if you want, or take a room at the inn." He pats my arm.

Beth soon joins us. She wraps her cardigan around her belly that doesn't quite stretch enough. "What's going on?" She looks worried as she comes up and puts her arm around me. "Are you okay?"

"Something happened with Ty."

She pulls out her phone and fires off a text message. "Okay, come on, we're going to meet up with Allie." She types more on her phone and then slides it back into her pocket and stands on her tip toes to kiss Evan. "Babe, can you keep the boys?"

"Yeah. It'll be okay, Mellie," he says as he leaves.

"Thanks." I follow Beth to the bunkhouse to pack.

She looks over at me. "Am I going to want to kill him?"

"I don't know. He lied to me. A big lie." My heart sinks again and I feel so distraught.

"Okay, well Allie is headed this way and she's bringing food. You look like hell, Mel. Is that grass in your hair? Tell us everything. We'll be Ty's judge and jury. And his executioner if we have to," she adds as she shoots me a fierce look.

We get out of the car and as soon as we get inside, Beth turns on the lights and falls onto the couch.

Allie pulls up moments later and comes in carrying a huge platter. "I wasn't sure what we needed, so I stole this whole snack board. I'll have to make a new one later, but it'll be worth it. Beth sent out a 911 for snacks and vent time."

I bite my lip to keep from crying and they both curl up with cozy blankets across from me to listen. Nova curls up next to me and I pet her, feeling calmer already.

I tell them everything and they don't say anything until I'm done. Finally, I say, "Well? What do you think?"

Both have wide eyes and look at each other. Beth says, "How did he look in that uniform?"

I roll my eyes. "Beth!"

Allie says, "On a scale of one to ten hotness, what do you rate the ATF costume?"

"It's not a costume. It's real. And he was hot, he's always hot," I admit. "But he lied. He never worked at Larkin. He's an ATF agent."

My whole past marriage was built on lies. I won't live like that with a man ever again, I don't care how much he loves us.

Allie says, "Okay, here's the facts. The Ty that we know? He's a good guy. He loves you and Kase. He would do anything for you. His job? Not as important."

"But the truth was important."

"Maybe he couldn't." Beth shrugs.

"Did you hear him out?" Allie asks.

"No. I didn't want to hear more lies."

"I think Evan's right. You need to at least see what he has to say. We can keep Kase so you can sort this out with him,"

Beth says.

"Bradley hurt me so much. I can't let anyone do that to me again. To us," I say honestly.

"Ty's not like that. He's one of us. He's good people," Allie says.

"I thought he was."

"He is. You have a right to be mad, but don't throw this away because of something he couldn't help. Wait until you hear all the facts from him, then make a decision."

I look down at my phone and there are three messages from Ty.

Ty: I love you.

Ty: I'm wrapping things up here.

Ty: I'm coming home. Where are you?

"He says he's on his way home. He said he loves me. I don't know what to say." I stand up. "Can you guys help me? I'm going to grab a few things and go to the garden shed for the night. I need to think. A lot has gone down the past few days... I just need time."

Beth stands, holding her belly. "I'll drop you off. I need to get back. You coming to get Caleb?" she asks Allie.

"Yes, let me get my coat. I'll bring these snacks to the inn and we can hang out for a while. I need to know what happens."

Feeling numb, I ride with Beth to the garden shed and

she drops me off. I feel like this can't be fixed. I don't know what to do next.

I don't want to lose him. But what if I never really had him?

CHAPTER 27

Ty

Fixing things is what I do.

It's over. The mission is over, and we finally took out a huge ring that was distributing dangerous Fentanyl to criminals all over the country from the Larkin factory. I feel relieved and stressed that this is over, as well as my career with the ATF.

I still don't know where Mellie and I stand. I couldn't have told her anything even if I wanted to. I'm not sure what everyone is going to think of me now, or if I'll be welcomed back around Freedom Valley or the inn, but I have to at least try to make things right.

I am a mechanic at heart, having grown up with my dad teaching me how to fix anything and everything. I'm a fixer. It's what I do. I don't know if I can fix what I broke with Mellie, but nothing is going to keep me from trying. I'll do anything to make it right. Somehow, they've become my entire world and I can't be without them now.

Special Agent Taylor approaches me and shakes my hand. "Are you sure you're making the right decision?"

"Never been more sure, sir." I shake his hand firmly.

"How can we thank you for your service? I know the past few years have been a sacrifice."

I think about it for a minute and say, "I do have one thing you could help me with."

"You can have whatever you want at this point. You name it. You've been an asset to the ATF."

I fill him in on the details of my request and then turn to head out. "Thank you," I call as I head over to my truck to make a few calls. I reach for my phone and text her. I just hope she gives me a chance to explain everything.

She texts me back, and my heart drops.

Mellie: I'm going back to the garden shed. I need some time, Ty.

Ty: Don't go. Please let me explain.

Mellie: Not tonight. I'm exhausted, and I need to think about everything.

Ty: Can we meet tomorrow?

Mellie: I don't know.

Mellie: And Ty?

Ty: What?

Mellie: I have Nova. Please don't make Kase give her back tonight. He's lost enough.

Ty: I love you both. This is not over.

Goddammit. I punch my steering wheel, and when I pull up to the bunkhouse, it's like I was on auto-pilot. I don't even remember driving here. I head in and drop my bag, the food still on the table that Mellie had been bringing me for dinner before I ripped her heart in two.

I just hope she gives me the chance to put it back together.

CHAPTER 28

Mellie

I did it once, I can do it again.

Beth drops me and Nova off with her trailing behind me before she runs up the stairs to the loft on top of the garden shed.

Evan follows behind me, carrying a sleeping Kase. He sets him on the freshly made bed and heads back out and nods.

I whisper, "Thank you," as he goes down the stairs quietly.

Nova covers my face with kisses and then immediately goes to curl into Kase.

I look around the loft, at what used to feel like home, and realize that it no longer is. But we can make it work again,

I tell myself. If there's one thing I'm good at, it's having to start over.

I did it once, I can do it again. It's just going to hurt a hell of a lot.

CHAPTER 29

Ty

She's going to have to
meet me halfway.

I wake up to my face being licked and forget where I am. I open my eyes and see Nova covering me excitedly in kisses. And yes, I did sleep on the floor of the laundry room in the garden shed. I couldn't help it. I missed them and wanted to be close to them.

"Ty," Kase says as he comes down the stairs. "You came to stay at the garden shed, too?" He looks confused, and I can't blame him.

"Just wanted to check in on you guys. I missed you," I say

as I stand and stretch. "Where's your mom?"

"She's coming. She's been sad. Did you come to make her happy?"

I wish it were that easy.

"Yes. Are you taking Nova outside?"

"Yeah, then we're going to go eat and Mom has to go to work," he says like it's every other day and our world didn't just shatter. Oh, to be four and not understand anything.

I climb the stairs and knock gently on the door jamb. Her head snaps over and her eyes are red-rimmed.

"What are you doing here?"

"I slept on your garden shed floor last night. I missed you guys."

Her mouth turns up a little, but as quickly as it appears, it disappears again. "I'm not ready to talk, Ty."

"Will you at least just listen to me, please?" I beg.

"How will I know what you're saying is true?"

"Because deep down you know."

"I don't know anything anymore, Ty."

"I love you both. You need time? Fine. I'll give you time. I'm not going anywhere. I live in the bunkhouse and I work for Sam Sr. full-time now. So, when you're ready, you come and find me," I say on my way out.

I love her, but she's going to have to meet me halfway.

CHAPTER 30

Mellie

You're stuck with us forever.

"I didn't expect that," I tell Sasha as I sip my coffee. "I didn't expect any of this."

"Wow, me neither," she says as I finish telling her everything. "So what are you going to do?"

"I don't know. It doesn't feel right in the garden shed. It doesn't feel like home anymore. Home was with Ty."

"It still can be, it sounds like," she says with a shrug of her shoulders.

I raise my eyebrows at her. "Not you, too."

"What?" she hedges. "I like Ty. I think he's good for you

and Kase. I heard your side, but I'm wondering what he has to say. Aren't you?"

"Maybe a little," I agree. My phone buzzes and I look down.

Ty: Can you meet me at the greenhouse tonight at dusk? I have something for you.

Mellie: What is it?

Ty: Just please be there. It's very important. You won't want to miss this.

Mellie: Fine. I'll text when I head that way.

Ty: I love you.

I start to say it back and then stop. I can't tell him that right now, not when I'm still pissed. It doesn't mean I don't still love him, though. I love him so much my chest aches. I want his arms around me so badly. I want him to tell me that it's going to be okay. But he broke something in me, and I can't tell if I'm too stubborn to fix it or if it's broken for good.

Maybe I need time on my own, so I can figure out for myself what my life is going to be.

Sasha refills my coffee and tops it off with cream. "It's going to be okay, honey. It's just a rough patch. You don't think Pete and I fight sometimes? We do. I know you like to think everything is peachy, but everybody has their issues."

I nod and take a sip of coffee. "I'm going to meet him tonight out by the greenhouse. He said he has something to show me."

"Oh? Well keep me posted."

"I will. Thanks, Sasha," I call as I take my mug and head to Evan's office at the front of the inn.

I knock and he says, "Come in."

"Hi," I say as I sit across from him at his desk.

"Did you talk to him?"

I shake my head. "Not yet. I'm meeting him tonight. Know anything about that?" I ask. Evan's face doesn't change, but I see it in his eyes. He knows. "What's he doing?"

"No clue," he says with a shrug, even though it's obvious that he does.

I get through my rooms, taking more time than usual. I'm exhausted and worn out. By the time I'm finished up, the shed door opens and Allie and Beth step in holding a bag.

"Hey, we're just here to help you freshen up before you go to meet Ty tonight," Beth says.

I narrow my eyes. "What do you two know?"

"Nothing," they say at the same time, too quickly.

"Right," I say dryly, putting the last load of towels on the linen cart.

"Come on, tell us the update while we do your hair. Let's go!" Beth steers me toward the stairs, kind of pushing me because I just want to go up there and drop to the bed and sleep for days.

But no, they make me shower, and when I come out, Allie starts on my hair with the blow dryer and Beth does my makeup.

"And why is this necessary?"

"Because you deserve to feel pretty and it might cheer you up," Beth says, adding some powder on my cheeks.

I can't argue with that, I do feel better already. I have on my new dark green overalls, my blonde hair falling in waves, and my makeup looks fresh and light, just the way I would have done it. When I look in the mirror, I see me, but who am I?

"What's the matter?" Beth asks, looking at me and back at Allie.

"I don't even know who I am anymore." I shrug.

"You're allowed to find out," Allie offers. "And you're always allowed to start over. You get to make the rules. It's your life."

I nod and stand. "Alright, I gotta get out there. Who wants to come with me?"

"I'll walk with you, but you'll be fine," Beth says, gathering up the makeup as Allie grabs her bag. "Come on, it's nice out."

It's getting dark, and I text Ty like I said I would.

Mellie: On my way.

Ty: I'm waiting. I love you.

I don't know why, but I have goosebumps. He stirs something in me that no one ever has before. He lied, but he still has my heart. Damn it.

I round the corner and I see that there are lights strung at the top of the greenhouse, illuminating it. "Wow," I say, suddenly feeling nervous. "That's pretty."

I see Ty standing in the lavender garden with two people I've never seen before. I head down the path toward them and Ty is smiling. He's with an older couple and I almost do a double take when I see that the man resembles an older version of Ty.

Holy shit. These are his parents.

His mom is smiling and she waves with one hand, holding something in the other. As I get closer, whatever she's holding is squirming. She kneels and sets something on the ground.

It's my dog. It's Sassy. I cover my mouth, tears filling my eyes.

"Sassy?"

She makes it to me, jumping and running in circles until I pick her up.

"My baby. How? Oh my God. Sassy..."

Ty comes up and stands in front of me, but his parents hang back.

"How did you do this? How did you get her?"

"I stole her when I went home last month, and my mom kept her until we could get her back to you. And I have two very important people I'd like for you to meet," he says nervously.

"Oh, Ty," I say as we walk toward them, holding Sassy who is licking my face and squirming, very happy to see me. His mom immediately pulls me into a hug.

"Hi, sweetie, it's so nice to finally meet you. I'm Tally, and this is Dale," she says, pointing to her husband who has a ball cap on just like his son usually does. He nods and smiles, his eyes matching Ty's, his almost identical beard with grey peppered through it.

"It's so nice to meet you both, too. I can't believe this. Thank you so much."

"Ty asked us to bring her. The ATF flew us up here as a favor to Ty for all his hard work on his case. It was a big one, and he worked so hard on it for so long."

"Mom..." he says, but he squeezes her arm gently, seeming nervous and embarrassed.

"Thank you so much. Really. I have worried about Sassy every day since we left."

"It's our pleasure, honey. She's a good dog, and she sure is happy to see you. I bet she'll like it here. Now, honey, show me these tomatoes I've been hearing about..." she says, pulling me down the path.

I look back to Ty and mouth, "Thank you."

Ty and I don't have a chance to talk, but I ride with them back to the inn so that he can drop his parents off there for the night. When Ty comes back out, I'm sitting by the firepit with Sassy, who is sprawled across my lap. I'm stroking her soft fur and I can't believe she's really here. Kase is going to be so happy.

Ty walks toward me hesitantly. "Can we talk now? Please."

"Yeah."

"Let's go home and talk."

We don't say anything as I follow him to the truck, as he opens the door for me, as we drive to the bunkhouse. The only sound is Sassy's elated panting.

We go in, and it still feels like home. He feels like home, despite everything that has happened. I set Sassy down to explore, and she sniffs and wags her tail.

I can't even look at him, I'm too nervous. I don't know what to say. He feels like a stranger to me right now, yet I still love him. Sometimes love isn't enough if you can't trust someone, though.

As always, he's in tune with what I'm thinking and feeling.

"I love you," he says softly.

"I feel like I don't even really know you. I don't know what's real and what's in my head," I say honestly.

"We're real," he says, kissing the top of my head. "We've

always been real. The only thing that wasn't real was my job at Larkin. I was an ATF agent working on a Fentanyl case that turned into a long assignment. It was never meant to go this long, but I'm so glad that it did. Otherwise, I wouldn't have met you and Kase."

I turn to look at him and he strokes Sassy's head. "I wanted to tell you, but I couldn't."

"Can you tell me everything now?"

"I'll tell you anything you want to know."

"Was Toad involved in any of this?" I ask, remembering that he worked at Larkin, too.

"No. The Eastern Bones were clean. In fact, they actually helped us. They didn't want that crap around here either."

"Where are you really from?"

"Alabama. That is all true."

"What's your real name?"

"Tyson Flynn Harden. And Nova is Nova," he says with a small smile.

"Where will you go now that this assignment is over?" I glance away, unwilling to watch his face as he lets me down.

"I'm staying here with you. I promise I'll never lie to you again. I didn't want to before, I hated every single minute of it."

I stare at him and know that he's telling the truth, so I give him the same. "Falling in love with you was unexpected, in the most beautiful kind of love. But you lied to me, and I don't know where we go from here."

He just nods and stares at me.

"Bradley shattered me, and I had to run away... but you make me want to run to you. Even when you lie. How are you still my safe space even after all of this?"

"Because what we have is real love. I love you both so much, Mellie."

"I love you too, Ty." I lay my head on his shoulder.

"You're the whole reason I believe that love really exists, Mellie. I promise to love you and Kase forever. You're it for me." His face is full of love and conviction as he says this.

"You think we can come back from all of this?" I ask.

"I know we can."

I lean in and kiss him, and he folds me into his arms. "I'm going to marry you, Mellie."

"I'm going to marry *you*."

"Oh, I'll be asking," he confirms, kissing me.

"I'm not moving to Alabama, though," I say.

He smiles and laughs. "Freedom Valley is home. I think we both know that." He looks at me, heat in his eyes, and picks me up and carries me into his room while kissing me.

He lays me down on his bed and kisses me until I forget I was ever mad at him. Breathless, I wrap my arms around him and kiss him back. He sits up to pull off his shirt and jeans, and it's honestly the hottest thing I've ever seen. I feel something so deep with him, something that I've never felt before. It's funny how we can fall in love with the most unexpected person at the most unexpected time and then you can't imagine living without them, no matter what their imperfections are or what happens.

He leaves his black boxer briefs on and turns on the lamp. "I want to see you, Mellie."

I sit up and pull my shirt off, his eyes never leaving mine. As soon as my overalls are off, he's on me, cradling me in his arms and pulling me into him sideways, kissing my face across my cheeks. "These freckles," he says. "I love them so much."

My freckles have always been something I've been self-conscious about. Bradley hated them and always wanted me to cover them up with makeup. He said I looked like a child. Whatever. These freckles are who I am, and hearing Ty say he loves them makes me feel better.

My hands wind their way down his chest, over his muscular stomach and down his boxers, finding him already hard for me. He groans into my ear slightly and kisses down my neck and across my chest.

"Do you forgive me, Mel?" he asks as his kisses trail down my stomach.

"I'm working on it," I tease.

"Work faster," he says, working his way down to my already wet center. In a flash, my panties are gone and he's working me with his tongue. I lean my head back and think about how good he makes me feel when I'm with him. But this? I need this. I need him.

I grip his shoulder as I come hard. He grabs a condom from his drawer and I watch him put it on, anxious to have him inside of me.

He enters me and says, "Mellie…"

"Yes…" I moan and he pounds harder, kissing me as he makes love to me, and I finally come hard, pulling him in closer to me and gripping his shoulders as I feel him shake and fall beside me, pulling me in close.

"Why haven't we done this sooner?" I gasp.

"Because I couldn't do it until you really knew. I needed you to know it was more than this. I'm in, Mellie. I want you and Kase to be my family. Forever. You're my forever, Mel," he says, kissing me again.

"Okay," I whisper.

"Okay," he whispers back.

"We still have so much to talk about," I murmur.

"We have time. We have forever."

I chuckle. "Yeah, we do."

"I have to tell you something," he says tentatively.

I sit up on my elbows and look at him. "What?"

"When you left, Mitch said something to you. What was it?"

"Why?" I ask, confused about what he means.

"I talked to him when I went to your old house. I went to

Diamond, and I took Sassy, and when I talked to Mitch, he said to tell you to remember what he told you. What was it?"

"Oh," I say, remembering. "He said it's absolutely okay to start over and let someone else love me the way I deserve."

I remember when he said that to me, I couldn't imagine loving again or finding someone to trust again. I thought it was just something he said, but now it means something.

Ty nodded. "It *is* okay, Mellie."

"Yeah. You really went to Diamond? Did you see Bradley?"

"I did see him from a distance, but I never talked to him."

"Oh my God, I can't believe it. How's Mitch?"

"He seemed okay. Like a solid guy. You can call him now, you know."

"I guess I can, can't I?" I say.

"I have one more question," he says, kissing my shoulder. "What?"

"Make me a husband and father, Mel. Please." He tilts his head and looks at me adoringly.

"Yes," I whisper. "You're stuck with us forever."

"There's nowhere else I'd rather be."

He kisses me again, pulling me into him, and I breathe in a sigh of relief. In his arms is where I want to stay.

Mellie

Turn the Paige.

Beth, Allie, and I are at the bakery catching up on life. Beth rubs her super swollen belly and looks happy despite probably being wildly uncomfortable beginning her last trimester. I don't envy her right now. Summertime and pregnant with twins has to be rough.

The door to the bakery opens and a short, red-haired woman comes in, looking like she's been crying. We stop talking and stare as she reaches into her bag and then looks over at where the napkins are kept. She heads over to the dispenser, takes a large wad out, and wipes her eyes.

Allie stands and approaches her. "Are you okay?"

The woman shakes her head. "No. No, I'm not. I'm sorry. I'm just having a really hard day."

Beth waves her over. "Come on over and join us. I'm Beth."

The woman looks at us tentatively, then nods. Allie pulls out a chair for her and she sits, letting her bag drop to the floor with a load thunk.

Allie looks down. "Geez, what do you have in there? Bricks?"

"No, books. I have my 'reading now,' my 'just read,' and a few back-up 'emergency' books." She wipes her eyes again.

Beth leans forward and says to us, "She's in," then she turns to the woman. "I'm an author. I get it. Books are everything."

The mystery redhead, who looks like a real-life Merida from *Brave*, now smiles even though she's clearly distraught about something.

"What happened?" Allie says, looking concerned.

"I just got to town and I leased a building for my bookstore. Apparently, it was all a scam. The scammer took my money and ran." She sniffs. "Now I can't open my shop here in town."

"Wait, do you own the new bookstore? Turn the Paige?" Beth asks excitedly.

"Yes, but now I can't open it thanks to this jerk. I put everything I had into that bookstore. Every last dime. I have no way to make a living now and nowhere to go."

"We could ask Preston to look into it," Beth suggests to the group.

The woman looks at us in disgust. "Preston Steele?"

"Yeah...?" Allie says, confused.

"He's the jerk who bought the building I rented!"

"Whoa," Beth says. "There must be some mistake. We can talk to him."

"You know him?" the desperate woman asks.

"Yeah," Allie says. "It doesn't sound like something he would intentionally do."

"Where are you staying?" I ask. While I'm usually the quiet one of the group, for some reason, I know I like this girl and I want us to help her.

"I have to put my inventory in storage. I'll be in my van until I can figure out a job and a place to stay while I save up again, file all my permits and find a new place to lease."

I mouth "garden shed" to Beth. She smiles and taps into her phone. I'm guessing she's texting Evan.

"Let's get you a sandwich and drink. My treat," Allie offers. "What would you like to drink?"

The woman sniffs and smiles. "I wouldn't turn down a vanilla latte. Thank you."

"Coming right up."

Beth's phone pings with a return text and she smiles. "You can stay in our garden shed. There's a little apartment on top of it. It's yours if you want it until you can get things sorted."

"You guys are doing too much. I want to say no, but honestly, I have nowhere to go." She looks desperate and sullen.

"We've all used the garden shed for a safe place to land from time to time. It's not far from here, at the Golden Gable Inn. Do you know where that is?"

"Yeah, I grew up here. My grandfather raised me. He lives in the Freedom Valley Assisted Living facility now. I moved back to open my shop to be near him."

"Oh, that's so sweet," Beth says, rubbing her belly, leaning forward for a cookie.

"I don't know how I'm going to open my shop now. This feels like it's over before it even began," Paige says, defeated.

"Don't worry, we'll talk to Preston," Beth says confidently.

"If anyone can fix anything, it's Preston." I smile at her. "Welcome back to Freedom Valley. I'm glad you're here.

FREEDOM VALLEY SERIES

Falling Inn Love

Baked Inn Love

All Inn Thyme

Love Inn Books (6.29.23)

Forever Inn Love (9.14.23)

Inn the End (11.30.23)

STANDALONES

The Firewatch Girl (TBD)

NON-FICTION

Writers Inspiring Writers with Jennifer Probst

ABOUT THE AUTHOR

Erin Branscom has read everything she can get her hands on for as long as she can remember. To this day, her favorite place is still the library. In 2021, after a decade of writing novels just for fun, she finally decided to finish a book series and has found writing novels to be her greatest escape. Erin is a passionate author's advocate and host of the highly popular My Level 10 Life podcast on Amazon Live, where she interviews authors live every week. She lives in Oklahoma and loves traveling and spending time with her husband, four kids, and best friend Molly, a Boston Terrier mix.

COME FIND ME:

Mailing list: bit.ly/3Z0QbV2
TikTok: www.tiktok.com/@mylevel10life
Amazon: www.mylevel10life.live
Bookbub: @erinbranscom
Goodreads: www.goodreads.com/mylevel10life
Facebook: www.facebook.com/erinbranscomauthor
Instagram: www.instagram.com/mylevel10life
Twitter: twitter.com/himylevel10life
Email: erin.branscom@gmail.com

ACKNOWLEDGEMENTS

Dusty, Kameron, Ethan, Audrey, and Charlotte, thank you for being the best family I could ever ask for. Thank you for always supporting me on my crazy adventures. I love you all so much!

Mom, thanks for reading my books and encouraging me. Also, thanks for letting me be born. You're the best mom.

Dad and Michael in heaven, I miss you both so much. Every day. It's not fair. I wish you were here. I hope I've made you proud.

Julie and Elizabeth, thanks for being great sisters. We've been through so much in the past few years. Our family is still standing strong.

Auntie Susan and Auntie Paula, you are the best aunt's anyone could ever ask for. I love you both so much.

Molly, you are my best friend in the entire world. Thanks for listening to me talk about all this book stuff and for always keeping me warm in my chair. You deserve all the bones and snuggles.

Brianna, I couldn't do it all without you! Thank you so much!

Erica, you're my favorite human. Period.

Kristi, your taco dates and brainstorming sessions mean the world to me. I'm so thankful for you and your friendship. Also, your success is so inspiring. You work harder than anyone I know!

Piper and Nora, let's make this our year! So thankful I found you two!

Willow, thanks for all of the sprints! You're so motivating and inspiring to me!

Enni (Yummy Book Covers), thank you for bringing Freedom Valley to life. I love all these covers so much! Thank you for all that you do!

Brooke Crites (Proofreading by Brooke), thanks for being a great editor.

To everyone reading this... Thank you for taking a chance on me and my Freedom Valley world.

STAY TUNED FOR...

Book #4 in the Freedom Valley Series,
Love Inn Books

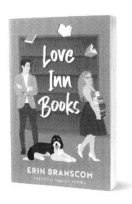

Coming 6.29.23

Pre-order on Amazon.

If you like enemies to lovers, bookstores,
and racoons, I've got you covered!